Drive

Drive

Eric Howling

James Lorimer & Company Ltd., Publishers
Toronto

James Lorimer & Company Ltd. acknowledges the support of the Ontario Arts Council. We acknowledge the support of the Government of Canada through the Book Publishing Industry Development Program (BPIDP) for our publishing activities. We acknowledge the support of the Canada Council for the Arts for our publishing program. We acknowledge the support of the Government of Ontario through the Ontario Media Development Corporation's Ontario Book Initiative.

Cover illustration: Steven Murray

The Canada Council | Le Conseil des Arts
for the Arts | du Canada

ONTARIO ARTS COUNCIL
CONSEIL DES ARTS DE L'ONTARIO

Library and Archives Canada Cataloguing in Publication

Howling, Eric, 1956-
    Drive / Eric Howling.

(Sports Stories)
ISBN 978-1-55277-010-8 (bound).—ISBN 978-1-55277-009-2 (pbk.)

    I. Title. II. Series: Sports stories (Toronto, Ont.)
PS8615.O9485D75 2008   jC813'.6   C2007-907514-2

James Lorimer & Co. Ltd.,	Distributed in the United States by:
Publishers	Orca Book Publishers
317 Adelaide Street West,	P.O. Box 468
Suite 1002	Custer, WA USA
Toronto, Ontario	98240-0468
M5V 1P9	
www.lorimer.ca	

Printed and bound in Canada.

CONTENTS

THE FRONT NINE

THE BACK NINE

For Flynn and Cooper

Acknowledgements

As a young boy growing up in Montreal, I would rise before dawn to sneak onto the local golf course with my friends Paul and Greg. Little did I know our shared sense of adventure would one day lead to a book. But it has. I'd like to thank Hadley Dyer at Lorimer for her initial interest in the story and Faye Smailes for her continued encouragement and steady editorial hand. I am indebted to Andrew Berzins for first igniting my interest in writing, to Paul Long for his unwavering support, and to my wife Julie for her daily inspiration. Finally, there are the many friends with whom I have shared unforgettable moments playing this great game. Play away.

1 Mission at Dawn

Bzz! Bzz! Bzz! The alarm was trying to pull Jake Cooper out of his deep sleep. Jake wanted to roll over and stop the buzzing. Instead, he lay there wondering why he felt so tired and why his room was so dark. Then he remembered — it was five o'clock in the morning. Jake reached over to push the off button and sat up on the edge of his bed, stretching his arms and yawning. It wasn't easy getting up before dawn, but he knew he had to. He had a mission.

He switched on the light and stumbled over to the clothes that were already waiting on the chair. He pulled on jeans, a white T-shirt, and an old grey sweatshirt. He crept down the hall past the bedroom where his mother still slept. Carrying his sneakers, he moved silently through the empty kitchen past the big yellow box of cereal left out on the counter for him. There would be time for breakfast later. Tugging on his blue cap, Jake slipped out the back door and into the waiting darkness.

He scrambled through the hedge to the house next door. He slid around the corner and stood under a bedroom window. Crouching down, he picked up a couple of small pebbles and threw them at the window. *Plink … plink* — they bounced off the glass. Suddenly, the curtain was pulled back by a pair of hands. It was Jake's best friend, Randy Robinson. Jake waved at him to come outside.

"Let's go!" Jake whispered.

The two boys raced along the sidewalk past the chain of small houses, each with their drapes drawn tightly. In a few short hours all the kids would be taking buses to school, and the moms and dads would be driving to the tall office buildings downtown. But now it was dead quiet and eerie. The boys darted under the street lamps that arched high over the road, just as they had so many mornings before.

At the end of their street Jake and Randy reached a field. They hiked across it until they came face-to-face with a chain-link fence. Hanging on it was an old wooden sign with big red letters that warned "PRIVATE PROPERTY — KEEP OUT!" But it was going to take more than a few red words to stop Jake and Randy. They climbed high above their heads and jumped over, landing softly on the other side. They were in.

Anyone watching might have seen them as two shadowy figures dashing along the edge of the fence.

They crouched low to keep out of view for as long as possible. Their running shoes were wet from the dew that lay heavy on the grass. They were getting close and soon their mission could begin.

There it was — the start of the thirteenth hole at the Royal Calgary Golf Club. For some members of the exclusive club, thirteen was an unlucky number, but it was Jake's favourite. A tall cedar hedge curved around them like a giant horseshoe. No one could see them there.

Jake remembered the first time he stood on this very spot three years before. He could still feel the rush of power that had surged through him after he made his first shot. Jake could hit a golf ball a lot farther than he could bat a baseball, throw a football, or shoot a hockey puck. He had never been very good at other sports, but swinging a golf club seemed natural.

He liked that golfers had their own lingo. They seemed to speak in a secret code. You didn't just hit the ball to start each hole, you "teed off" with a "drive" from the "tee box." You didn't just tap the ball into the hole, you made a "putt" into the "cup." When you hit the ball from the grass, you say you made your shot from the "fairway." And when you took the right number of shots to play a hole you didn't just make a good score, you made "par." There were lots of other cool golf words too — for the types of clubs, like irons, woods, putters; for the scores for each hole, like bogey, birdie, and eagle — and Jake learned them all.

Jake could play this hole in his sleep. The thirteenth hole was 400 yards long, and bent to the left in what was called a "dogleg." Poplar trees lined both sides of the fairway — leafy giants that had been growing for nearly a hundred years. There was a single sand trap craftily placed 200 yards out, an early hazard that you had to miss with your drive. The green lay another 200 yards away, guarded by three more large sand traps just waiting to gobble up your ball. It was a tough par four — you were supposed to get the ball from the tee into the hole in four shots — but it was fair. Jake knew that, one by one, good shots would always be rewarded with a good score.

As the boys pulled out their golf balls they could see the first glimmers of dawn break into the sky. Long streaks of red and orange reached through the inky blue like twisted witch fingers.

"Who are you going to be?" Jake asked, knowing full well which famous golfer Randy liked to pretend he was.

"Tiger," said Randy, without having to add the last name *Woods*. "How about you? Phil Mickelson ... Ernie Els ... Sergio Garcia?

"Nope, I'm going with Mike Weir today. He's Canadian and I'm Canadian. He's got a smooth swing and I've got a smooth swing. He won the Masters tournament and I — "

"You what?"

"I'm *going* to win a tournament, some day."

"Dream on," Randy laughed.

Jake chose his three-iron, one of only three clubs he had brought on the morning mission. Jake's clubs were old, with nicks and cuts in the steel blades, but he couldn't afford new ones. He had been lucky to find these at a garage sale. He also carried a nine-iron and a putter. Jake and Randy travelled light so they could play fast — and run fast, if they had to. They never knew what danger lay around the next corner.

The two boys took a few practice swings to warm up before playing their first shots. Jake dragged the club back lightly along the grass to make sure the arc of his swing was as big as it could be. That's what it said to do in *How to Play Like a Pro,* the big golf book Jake kept borrowing from the school library. He always made sure he followed the instructions written inside "to a tee." Jake laughed to himself at the cornball joke.

"It's your honour." Randy broke the silence. "You beat me last time, so you hit first."

"Yeah, I sank that amazing long putt to win, didn't I?" Jake rubbed it in for all it was worth.

Jake took his stance so that he could comfortably reach the ball with his three-iron. He planted his feet the same width as his shoulders and bent his knees. After lightly gripping his club he pulled the shaft back, turning his wrists during the backswing. Then he unleashed a powerful downward motion, his arms and legs all shifting forward, to strike the ball with a crisp *thwack!*

The ball fired off the clubface and sailed straight and true, rising into a high arc before landing softly on the grass in the middle of the fairway.

"Great shot!" Randy shouted.

"Not bad for first thing in the morning," said Jake, smiling again. "You're up."

Jake stood back and watched his friend get ready for his drive. Even when lining up a shot, Randy had an easy-going grin that matched the way he played the game. He never got mad if he hit a bad shot. He had fun no matter what his score was.

After looking down the fairway, Randy concentrated again on the ball. When he swung, the ball jumped off his three-iron and soared down the fairway, rolling to a stop about 10 yards short of Jake's.

"Nice ball," Jake said. He was impressed, as Randy rarely hit as far as he did.

Jake and Randy marched down the fairway counting the yards as they went.

"One-sixty-three … " Jake said.

"One-sixty-four … " Randy continued.

"One-sixty-five … " Jake finished as he took the last step to Randy's ball.

"Pretty good for a couple of three-irons," Randy chirped.

"Pretty good for a couple of up-and-coming pros who play in secret," Jake added.

Randy played next, as he was farther from the green. Randy's second shot slid off his clubface and skidded through the grass.

"That's okay. One more good one and you'll be on the green," said Jake.

"No problem," said Randy.

Jake still had 225 yards left to the hole. He needed to hit another long shot with his three-iron, and then a short chip shot with his nine-iron to the green. But it wasn't a straight path to the hole. Jake would have to hook it left around the dogleg. He adjusted his stance and his grip, then hit his second shot with an easy, fluid swing. The ball soared gracefully around the corner, landing about 50 yards in front of the green, which was shaped like a giant kidney bean.

Randy picked up his nine-iron and swung with just half his strength. The ball flew high into the air, landing gently on the green about 30 feet to the right of the flagstick that marked the hole. Jake's chip shot landed a little closer to the hole, but his ball was on the left side.

"Sink these and we both make par-fours," Jake said, his green eyes flashing. "You're away." Jake let Randy go first because his ball was a little farther from the flag. Randy hunched over his putt, taking a few practice swings before gently pulling back his putter and stroking the ball. It rolled smoothly across the green, coming to a stop just before it reached the cup. He walked over and knocked it in.

"Nice bogey!" said Jake.

"I'll take it." One over par was a good score for Randy.

Then it was Jake's turn. He liked to pretend it was the final hole of the Masters tournament and he had to sink the putt into the hole to win. Jake imagined a huge crowd of spectators watching him as he stood over his putt, casting a long, thin shadow across the green. He squatted down behind the ball to better judge how it would bend on the way to the hole. He knew the slope of the green would make it break a bit to the left. So Jake aimed a bit to the right of the hole. The ball rolled off the blade of his putter, moving first to the right, then curving back toward the cup. It had just enough speed to … drop … in — *plunk!* Jake raised his putter high in the air to celebrate his make-believe tournament victory.

"Just another easy par-four for Jake Cooper!" Randy laughed.

The two friends played three more holes before they looked at their watches and saw that it was time to go. The sun was rising in the sky, and soon the Royal Calgary staff would be arriving to cut the fairways. Jake and Randy didn't want their mission to end with them getting caught, so they picked up their clubs and headed for home. They still had to eat breakfast and go to school.

As they trudged back to the fence, they saw a single black car wind slowly down the long driveway toward the huge clubhouse. The two boys raced to the fence, quickly scrambled up and over, then dove behind some bushes to hide. Their hearts pounded as they peered through the leaves. They watched a tall man open the front door and step out. He was dressed all in black to match his car. He wore a black golf shirt, black pants, and black sunglasses that hid his eyes so Jake and Randy couldn't tell where he was looking. Maybe he was staring right at them!

The man pulled a heavy black golf bag out of the trunk, slung it over his shoulder, and walked with long strides over to the driving range. Jake and Randy looked at each other, wondering *Who is he? What is he doing? And why is he up so early?* Then they ran.

2 Locker Talk

Brriiing! The big red bell above Jake's locker rang loudly to signal the start of another school day. Jake stifled a yawn. If it wasn't the alarm buzzing to wake him up, it was the bell ringing to let him know classes were about to begin in just five minutes.

Jake spun the numbers to his combination and swung his locker open, ready for another long day at Evergreen Junior High. Jake was no Einstein, but he worked hard. He had to do well because of the deal he had made with his mom. She told Jake over and over again, "If you don't get good grades, you don't get to golf." He had to get good grades.

Now that the warm June weather had finally arrived, there was only one more week to survive. Jake still had a bunch of homework and some tests, but then the summer holidays would officially start. He couldn't wait.

It's not that Jake hated school, he just hated the

person who had the locker right next to his. Less than an arm's length away was Tyler Justin Davis II, loudmouth extraordinaire.

"Did we play great on Sunday, or what?" Tyler Justin made sure everyone in the hall could hear him.

TJ was always bragging about what a great golfer he was. TJ was a member of Royal Calgary, along with his rich friends Brandon, Ryan, and Zach. They called themselves the Fearsome Foursome.

"First time we all broke 100," Brandon said boastfully of his score for all eighteen holes.

"We were hitting that driver a mile!" TJ said, pretending to swing an invisible club.

"And right down the middle every time," Ryan added.

"I don't think anyone could have beaten us yesterday," TJ said, shaking his head.

Jake knew that, unlike TJ and his friends, he could never afford to play at Royal Calgary — or at any other golf course, for that matter — except by sneaking in. So he kept his mouth shut. His mom always told him that if you couldn't back up what you said, it was better to say nothing at all. Still, he would love to play against the Fearsome Foursome one day, just to show them how the game was really played.

The Foursome all high-fived each other, picked up their books, shut their lockers, and walked right past Jake without saying a word. Jake knew they thought that, if you weren't a golfer, you weren't worth talking to. And as far as they were concerned, Jake wasn't a golfer. But Jake didn't want anyone knowing about his secret morning missions, at least not yet.

Jake felt like he was invisible today, which was just fine with him. Most days, TJ would make fun of him — or worse. Jake still had a big purple bruise on his arm where he was slammed against his locker the week before. Watching the Foursome walk away meant he had escaped trouble. Jake took a deep breath.

Making sure TJ was a safe distance away, Jake rolled his eyes at Randy, whose locker was on the other side of his. Whether it was at school or home, it was good to know Randy was always right next door. He wondered how he could have such a good friend on one side and such a jerk like TJ on the other.

Before Jake could close his locker and make a quick get-away, he heard TJ yelling, "Hey, Junkyard Jake!" TJ couldn't leave without getting a shot in. "Nice threads! Get your clothes out of a dumpster?" Everyone in the hallway turned to stare at Jake. Brandon, Ryan, and Zach all burst out laughing.

Jake knew he looked shabby in his jeans and old T-shirt, but it was all his mom could afford. She didn't earn the kind of money that other rich parents made working in the oil business. The strange thing was, even when his mom had a few extra dollars and offered to buy Jake new clothes, he said he didn't need any. What was the point of wearing new clothes? He would still get picked on.

Jake wanted to cram himself in his locker and pull the door shut. But he just stood there until TJ and his posse lumbered away down the hall. "Are you going to the camp?" Jake heard Brandon ask TJ as they passed a hand-painted poster for a summer science camp in the Rocky Mountains. "Looks like it might be a good time."

"Are you kidding?" TJ scoffed. "The summer is for one thing and one thing only — golf. Who's got time to go and learn about experiments and scientific stuff like that?"

"Right." Brandon quickly changed his tune, and jogged to keep up with the much taller TJ. "Who needs it?"

TJ and his gang thought they were the coolest four guys at school. Jake was used to seeing them march down the crowded hall side-by-side like a small army, all wearing brand new khaki pants and white golf shirts with the red Royal Calgary logo, expecting the other kids, and even teachers, to move out of their way. What always surprised Jake was how everyone ran for cover. He wasn't the only one intimidated by the Fearsome Foursome.

What Jake really resented was that they had the money to do whatever they wanted, whenever they wanted. But, even though he told Randy he hated the

Fearsome Foursome, some small part of him secretly wished he could join their club. Jake knew they were jerks, but they were rich jerks. Maybe having big allowances was worth the trade-off.

Jake and Randy headed into math class, being careful to stay behind the Foursome, out of their sights. Their teacher, Mr. Dunnford, stood at the front of the classroom, writing some numbers on the blackboard. His bald head shone brightly under the fluorescent lights.

"Can anyone solve for x?" Mr. Dunnford turned and wrote $2x + 8 = 260$ on the board. Jake thought he knew the answer right away but was afraid to give it. The last thing he needed was to make a mistake and have the whole class laugh at him. Jake looked over and saw TJ's hand shoot into the air. *Uh oh,* he said to himself.

"I can!" TJ shouted.

"Yes, Mr. Davis?" Mr. Dunnford said.

"What *you* would shoot on a round of golf!" TJ blurted out.

TJ looked around the class for a reaction. And he got it — the kids exploded with shrieks and howls of laughter!

"Just let me know if you need lessons. I'm available Tuesdays," TJ added, pulling more snickers from the class.

Jake had to admit TJ had got the best of Mr.

Dunnford this time. Shooting 126 would be a pretty bad score. Mr. Dunnford looked upset, even hurt. He was surprised to realize that even a teacher could get bullied. He felt sorry for Mr. Dunnford, even though he didn't particularly like him. The class could always count on TJ for a good joke, especially about golf. But what could you do when the joking went too far?

3 Quack! Quack!

When he woke up, it seemed to Jake that he had been working on his science project only a few hours before. It seemed like that, because it had been only a few hours. He had stayed up past midnight writing about the planets of the solar system. He had written about how there are only eight, now that astronomers had looked through their high-powered telescopes and discovered that Pluto was just too small to count as a real planet. He liked that this discovery had been made during his lifetime — sometimes he felt that everything else had already been figured out, and he wanted to feel like he was part of something new.

Jake had finished describing the four planets farthest from the sun — Neptune, Uranus, Saturn, and Jupiter — but he still had to research the four inner planets of Mars, Earth, Venus, and Mercury. Luckily, he had one more day to complete everything before handing in the assignment to his science teacher.

Jake had chosen the topic for his project because he thought it was cool he could watch the solar system both night and day. Some nights he lay on the grass in the backyard and used a pair of old binoculars to observe the moon and the planets. He'd take a flashlight and an astronomy book that showed him where to look for each planet in the night sky. And every morning he got up to golf, he got to watch the sun come up. Jake knew that if he didn't get up early enough, he wouldn't be seeing that giant glowing ball rise over the trees on the thirteenth hole.

As Jake put on his clothes he looked at the pictures he had cut out of golf magazines and taped to the wall. All his heroes stared back at him — Mike, Tiger, Phil, Ernie, and Sergio. Jake knew what they'd be saying if they were really here.

"Get going, you lazy dog. You don't get to be a champion by staying in bed. There's only one way to get better — practise."

"I know, I know," Jake muttered to himself as he tiptoed down the hall, through the kitchen, and out the back door. He was tired. Between schoolwork and golf, he wasn't getting enough sleep, but he figured he could handle it. He didn't have the advantages that the Fearsome Foursome had. If he was going to be a pro one day, he had to work harder.

Randy was already waiting for him in the dark. It was a cool morning and a green golf cap was pulled down tight over his ears to keep him warm.

"Where have you been?" Randy whispered. "I was here at least ten minutes ago!"

"I've been talking with some friends," Jake replied.

"I hope you don't tell anyone else that you talk to your posters." Randy grinned. "Come on, let's go."

The two friends clutched their clubs and hurried down the quiet street. In a few minutes they had climbed the fence and were standing on the thirteenth tee box.

Jake took a deep breath, filling his lungs with the crisp air. He could relax out here on the golf course. Walking down the peaceful green fairways, he didn't have to listen to his mom fretting, wonder if his dad would ever come back home, or watch out for TJ and the Fearsome Foursome. With no one around but Randy, he could just be himself.

"Do you ever wonder what it would be like to be a hawk or a big black raven, and just fly out of sight?" Jake asked.

Randy stared at his friend like he was crazy, but instead of laughing at him, he just let it go. "Yeah, sometimes I do," admitted Randy.

Both boys took some practice swings to loosen up. Jake had decided to use two clubs, hoping the extra weight would make him a little more flexible. He held the three- and nine-irons together in his cold hands and swung in big, slow arcs. He was as ready as he was ever going to be.

"Are you going to hit, or just take practice swings all day?" Randy teased him.

Jake pulled a ball out of his pocket and stuck it on top of a tee in the grass. He stepped back, took one more easy practice swing with just his three-iron, then stood over the ball and swung for real. Jake expected the ball to launch smoothly and sail down the middle of the fairway like it usually did. But this morning it didn't.

Maybe it was the late night working on his science project. Or maybe it was the famous golf faces on his wall scolding him for not practising more. Whatever it was, the ball never got airborne. Then it curved left to go screaming into the woods.

"What the heck was that?" Jake yelled.

"That, my friend, is what's commonly known as a duckhook." Randy grinned.

"A duckwhat?" Jake was still in shock from seeing his ball dive into the trees.

"Your ball took off low to the ground then flew left into the bushes just like a duck," Randy explained. "Remember the description in *How to Play Like a Pro*?"

"I've seen golfers score birdies and eagles, but I've never seen ducks," Jake said. "And I hope I never see one again."

Then it was Randy's turn. He hit his ball smack in the middle of the clubface and sent it sailing down the middle of the fairway.

"Nice shot." Jake was glad when Randy played well, but he wished it was his ball instead.

Knowing that his first ball was probably lost in the thick bushes, Jake pulled a second ball out of his pocket and prepared to play another tee shot. This time things would be different. *Jake Cooper doesn't hit two bad shots in a row*, he said to himself.

He took a little more time, made three easy practice swings, breathed deeply, then stepped up to the ball and swung. *Thwack!* Jake looked up quickly, expecting to watch his ball soar down the fairway. But that's not what he saw. Another duckhook spun wildly to the left and flew straight into the bushes!

"Quack, quack!" Randy teased gently.

"I can't play anymore," Jake said, shaking his head.

"Sure you can. You're just having a bad day."

"No, I mean I only brought two balls, so I can't play anymore."

Randy gave Jake his second ball. After Jake finally hit a drive that landed in the fairway, the boys walked in silence to where they would take their second shots.

"I don't get it. What's wrong with my swing? I'm doing the same thing I always do," Jake said. He was pretty sure he was doing it just like the pictures showed in *How to Play Like a Pro*.

"Maybe you need more sleep," suggested Randy.

"Maybe you should mind your own business." Jake felt more frustrated than ever. He thought he knew the real reason for his bad play. It wasn't that he was staying up late doing homework, or that he was being picked on at school. All he needed was a lesson. Not from a book but from a person — a real pro.

Jake continued to struggle on the two holes they played after his crazy duckhooks from the thirteenth tee. Most days he wanted to play more, but that morning he didn't mind the thought of a quick bowl of cereal then heading off to school.

The sun had been up for an hour by the time the boys finished putting on the fifteenth green. They were about to make the walk back to the fence when they saw the mysterious black sedan parked near the driving range.

"Hey, Jake, there's that black car again," Randy said, nodding in the direction of the sleek black vehicle.

"It's a BMW." Jake recognized his favourite make. "And no ordinary Bimmer, either. It's a 750i with over 300 horsepower."

"That's one sweet ride. Let's go have a look."

"I don't know," Jake said cautiously.

"Come on!" Randy cried, his legs starting to move a little faster. "We'll be careful."

Jake and Randy sprinted to the edge of the fairway where they would be hidden by trees. They darted between the spruces until they were standing at the edge of the parking lot. The black sedan sat motionless. There was no one in sight.

"Okay. Closer," Randy said eagerly.

"Just for a minute, though." Jake was still not sure if it was safe. He dropped his clubs on the grass and walked slowly over to the car. Even though he knew he shouldn't, Jake couldn't resist darting his hand out to touch the famous blue, black, and white BMW symbol on the front hood. But he pulled his hand away just as quickly as he touched it. The hood was still hot from the engine! That meant the car had been sitting there only a few minutes. And that meant ...

"Nice car, eh, boys?" A man had suddenly appeared right behind them. He had approached as silently and invisibly as a ghost.

4 Caught!

Jake and Randy froze as stiff as a couple of flagsticks. They wanted to run but their legs wouldn't go. They tried to talk but their lips wouldn't move. All that came out of their mouths was, "Uh, huh."

"It's a BMW, you know," said the stranger.

"I know," said Jake. Why did he say that? They weren't even supposed to be here, and here he was sounding like a know-it-all.

"Go ahead and have a look. It was given to me quite a few years ago, but she still handles like a race car."

Jake and Randy slowly turned around to look at the man as he spoke. Jake imagined how he would feel if he found a couple of kids hanging around his fancy ride, but the man didn't sound angry. In fact, he almost seemed friendly, which was a good thing because he was huge. Jake and Randy came up to about his chest.

"We weren't going to do anything to your car," Jake said softly. "We just thought it looked cool."

"Oh, I know. It's a nice car — who could blame you?" The man shrugged.

Jake was just about to breathe a huge sigh of relief when the man said, "I see you've got some golf clubs with you."

Jake prepared for the worst. Royal Calgary was for members only, and they shouldn't be on the grounds, let alone be playing on the course. They had been caught red-handed! How much trouble were they in? Was this guy a staff member who would report them?

"We just played a couple of holes before anyone got here," Jake said quickly.

"We'll never do it again. Please don't turn us in," Randy pleaded.

The man crossed his arms and stared at their guilty faces. "Do you guys know who I am?" When the boys shook their heads, he continued. "My name is Cliff Spencer and I'm the head professional here at Royal Calgary."

Jake winced, and he could hear Randy gulp. The head pro was the most important person at the club. He had the power to do whatever he wanted.

"Here's what I've decided to do," said Cliff Spencer. Jake held his breath. What kind of punishment would they get for their trespassing? "I'm going to let you keep playing. But it has to be a secret just between us. I don't want you telling anyone or I could get in trouble."

Jake shot a quick glance over at Randy. Did he really hear what he thought he heard? Would they actually have permission to play on the course? Jake could see the shock and confusion he was feeling mirrored in Randy's face.

"I remember being your age and not being able to afford to play anywhere," explained the golf pro, answering the questions in Jake's head. "I had to sneak onto a nearby course, too. But that was back east in Ontario, and a really long time ago."

Jake couldn't believe their good luck. He and Randy could barely stutter out their thanks as they shook Cliff Spencer's hand. Then they turned to rush home before the hulk could change his mind.

"One more thing." Cliff Spencer's voice stopped them in their tracks. The boys spun around nervously.

"I noticed that you had a small problem duckhooking the ball on number thirteen, uh … ?"

"Jake," said Jake. "And this is Randy, Mr. Spencer."

"Well, Jake and Randy, what about I meet you both here at the driving range exactly one week from today? I can help you straighten that duckhook, and tackle some other little problems, too."

Jake and Randy raced for home, past the big clubhouse soon to be filled with rich oil executives; down the eighteenth fairway, where TJ and the Fearsome Foursome had played "so great" on the weekend; across the thirteenth tee box where Jake had hit two bad duckhook drives; all the way to the metal fence where the "PRIVATE PROPERTY — KEEP OUT!" sign hung. By the time they reached the safety of their street both boys were gasping for air. But it was all worth it. They would be a little late for school, but they didn't care. They were allowed to play at Royal Calgary and they were going to get a free lesson — from a real pro!

5 Like a Big Red Balloon

"Was that you singing in the shower?" Jake's mom asked as he ran into the kitchen, sliding along the slippery white linoleum floor.

"Did I sound like a famous rock star?" Jake slid right into his seat at the table.

"Well, now that you mention it, you did," said his mom, trying not to crack a smile.

"Then it *was* me." Jake's grin widened when he saw the pancakes on his plate. "You got up early to make these? Thanks!"

"I'd make pancakes for you every morning, if I didn't have to rush off to the Food Mart." Jake could hear the regret in his mom's voice and sighed. He wished that she didn't feel so guilty about not being able to buy him new golf equipment or not being around to spend more "quality time" with him. But Jake couldn't keep the ear-to-ear smile from his face for long, and his mom noticed right away.

"Did anything special happen today?"

"Oh, not really," Jake replied, topping his stack of steaming pancakes with maple syrup and digging in. "Unless you think having the head pro at Royal Calgary let you play on the course and offer you a lesson is special!"

"What? How did that happen?" The tone of her voice got suddenly serious. "Here I am worrying that I'll have to pick you up at the police station one of these mornings, and you're being rewarded for trespassing!"

"We're not really allowed to play," Jake said, putting down his fork. "Not like members or anything. But Cliff, uh ... Mr. Spencer said that Randy and I could keep using the course in the morning as long as we don't tell anyone."

"And what about the lesson? How much is that going to cost?"

"Nothing. He said it would be free." Jake picked up his fork again.

"Have you talked to this man before? What do you know about him? Who is he?"

"He seemed like a nice guy," Jake said around a mouthful of partially chewed food. "At first we weren't sure, because he snuck up on us while we were checking out his car. We thought we were in big trouble, but he wasn't mad or anything. That's when he invited us back next week for the lesson."

"It seems a little odd that he wants to give you a free lesson."

"I think he felt sorry for me after seeing the two terrible drives I hit straight into the woods."

"Well, I'm not sure you should go." Her voice sounded much more certain than her words. "You're doing just fine, learning from your golf book and playing with Randy."

Jake had to talk fast, before she actually told him he couldn't go. "Every time someone promises to do something nice for me, you always think they're going to back out, or that it's not going to work out."

"I don't want you to be disappointed," said his mom.

Jake knew his mother's worries had to do with his father's leaving them a couple years before. Jake's dad had told him that his marriage to Jake's mom was like a big red balloon. At the beginning it was blown up, but every year a little air leaked out until, finally, the balloon was flat and empty. After making this weird speech, he had handed Jake a letter filled with the usual sappy stuff — it said he would call every week, write every month, and visit whenever he could.

In the first few months, Jake had received a couple of letters. But as time went on, the arrival of the envelopes got further and further apart. As for the phone calls and visits, they never took place at all. Jake wondered if it was his fault, no matter how much his mom said that it wasn't, but he couldn't figure out what to do differently. It had been almost a year since he had received any word from his father. Jake didn't write letters to his dad anymore, because he didn't get anything back.

As he sat at the table stuffing pancakes into his mouth, thinking about his dad, Jake realized that his mom might be right about Cliff. Why would Cliff offer to help? Would Cliff really keep his promise and show up for the lesson? Maybe it *was* a little crazy, and too good to be true.

One thing Jake did know was that the school bus would be stopping just down the street in about two minutes. He raced back down the hall to brush his teeth, comb his hair, grab his backpack, and bolt out the front door — all in 120 seconds. It was a new record.

6 You Can't Judge a Book

Jake hurried to his locker and switched his social studies book for his science project. He was in a rush to meet Randy so he took off down the crowded hall, through the cafeteria that smelled like French fries, past the gym that smelled like stinky running shoes, and over to the library that smelled like old books.

The hall buzzed with activity every step of the way. Classes had just ended for the day and kids were running left and right to escape the school. There was lots of talking, laughing, and locker slamming, and some mostly good-natured pushing and shoving by the jocks on the football team. Then something amazing happened. As soon as Jake walked through the library door, all the racket that the hundreds of kids made suddenly came to a complete stop. He had walked into a giant bubble of silence.

Jake couldn't even hear the sound of his own footsteps as he shuffled along the green carpet, scanning the room for Randy. He walked past aisle after aisle of books, and row after row of kids doing their homework. Randy was nowhere to be seen.

"Pssst, I'm over here." Randy was sitting at a study booth near the back, far away from Mrs. Lindsay, the hawk-eyed librarian.

Jake sat down beside his friend and spread his science project out on the wooden table in front of him.

"You still have homework?" Randy whispered, shaking his head. "I finished mine hours ago."

"More like a minute ago," Jake laughed, quietly.

"We have to talk about our golf lesson," said Randy, doodling all over his geometry. "You know, here in secret — so TJ doesn't find out."

"Don't you think it's a little weird the golf pro said he'd give us a lesson?" asked Jake, frowning. "Man, it would suck if he didn't show."

"What are you talking about? He didn't have to tell us that he was going teach us, so he wouldn't have said it unless he wanted to do it."

"I guess you're right." Jake was still not totally convinced. Randy always had a more positive spin on things than Jake did. Jake liked that about him. It seemed whenever Jake was down, Randy was up. Jake wondered if it was because Randy's dad had a good job as an electrician. They always had enough money to do fun things, like going to Calgary Flames hockey games and eating at restaurants. *If I got to do that, I'd be in a good mood too*, he thought.

After talking about the lesson, Jake spent the next half hour writing down facts about Mercury, the last planet he had left to describe. "If I was on Mercury," Jake said to Randy, reading from his book, "I would weigh less than 15 kilograms." Randy didn't look up from his doodles. *I wonder how far I could hit a golf ball on Mercury*, thought Jake as he wrote, "Mercury is a lot smaller than Earth and would have less gravity to hold me down."

Once he finished the last page of his astronomy project, Jake decided it was time for a reward.

"Where are you going?" Randy whispered, watching Jake put down his pen and stand up.

"Be back in a flash."

Jake disappeared around the corner and headed for the sports section. He got to aisle five and ran his finger down the row of books until he found what he was searching for.

"Bingo!" Jake whispered as he pulled out a big green book. It had a picture of a golfer hitting a monster drive on the cover. Jake figured he must have pulled the well-worn book off the shelf and signed it out of the library a hundred times.

"Jake, why don't you try another book?" Mrs. Lindsay's face was peering at him from the other side of the shelf through the hole caused by his removal of the book.

"Mrs. Lindsay, you scared me." Jake tucked *How to Golf Like a Pro* under his left arm.

"How about this? Every time you borrow this book, you also have to borrow another."

She poked around on the shelf and presented him with a thick book of stories on the Roman Empire. He rolled his eyes and took it, then scurried back to the table.

"Of course," Randy said, eyeing the dog-eared golf book. "But remember, we have to be careful. We don't want you-know-who seeing us."

"Don't worry, I have a plan." Jake cracked open their favourite book and hid it inside the pages of the huge astronomy book. "Besides, what could happen here in the library? The Fearsome Foursome would never set foot in a library."

No sooner were the words out of Jake's mouth than he heard a familiar voice.

"Look! A couple of geeks sitting in the library! What a surprise!"

It was TJ and the rest of the Fearsome Foursome, standing just an aisle away. *What are they doing here?* wondered Jake. *They should be climbing into fancy European cars driven by their personal chauffeur mothers, not here doing homework they were too cool to do, in the library they were too cool to spend time in.*

"Doesn't look like you're doing much studying, Junkyard Jake," TJ taunted, crossing his arms and trying his best to look tough.

"Have you ever even been golfing?" Ryan asked, pointing at the big book that was still open in front of Jake and Randy.

"When school's out next week, that's all we'll be doing." TJ puffed out his chest and looked side-to-side at his three friends.

"Yeah, instead of reading about golf, we'll be playing," Brandon bragged.

TJ reached over and grabbed the two books out of Jake's hands. "This astronomy book is exactly what I need for my report, Junkyard. Thank you. And this golf book looks good. I think I'll take them both."

TJ waved the books in front of Jake's face. "Let's go, guys. We've got some reading to do."

Jake silently watched the Fearsome Foursome walk out of the library. He looked at his pitiful Roman Empire book and put his head on the table.

"I'd like to say something back to him one time, you know? But what could I say? I can't tell them that we're sneaking onto the course, or that we met a real golf pro."

"Jake, don't worry about it," said Randy. "We have to just let it go today, so we can keep playing golf tomorrow."

7 Left Behind

Almost a whole week — that's how long Jake had to wait for their lesson with Cliff Spencer. Six days ... or 144 hours ... or 8,640 minutes — not that Jake was counting or anything.

Jake tried to keep busy to make the time go by faster. He studied for his final social studies test on the history of Europe. He helped his mom cook spaghetti and meatballs twice in one week. He even cracked open the Roman Empire book Mrs. Lindsay forced on him. And, of course, he played golf with Randy every morning except Sunday.

On Sunday, he slept in until the sun woke him up. Jake thought it had to be noon but, when he squinted at his clock radio to check the time, it was only 7:12. Still, Jake hadn't climbed out of bed that late in months. Some days he felt dead tired, but it wasn't like he had a choice. If he ever wanted to be a pro golfer, he had to work hard — at golf and at school. His mom worried about his health, but he told her that he got more sleep than he actually did, when he thought he could get away with it.

Finally, it was Wednesday. Not only was it lesson day, it was also the last day of school. It was a perfect double whammy!

Jake turned off his alarm and turned on the silver reading lamp that snaked out from the wall above him. He lay there for a minute before rolling out of bed and putting on his clothes. He had laid out his jeans, white T-shirt, and red sweatshirt the night before. He wanted to make sure he wasn't late. He had chosen blue, white, and red because they were the official colours of Royal Calgary. *Man, if the Fearsome Foursome knew I was doing this, they'd bug me for sure*, thought Jake.

Jake downed a quick glass of orange juice from the fridge and slid over to the back door. He picked up his three old clubs, then quietly opened the door and stepped outside, expecting to see Randy waiting for him. Randy wasn't there.

Jake crept around the bushes to the far side of the house next door. Usually he could see the light on in Randy's bedroom, but not this morning. Jake picked up a couple of small pebbles and tossed them at the dark window, hoping to wake up his friend. Nothing stirred except the silly cowboy curtains covered with hats and boots that were blowing in the breeze through the bottom of the open window.

Jake started to panic. What if Randy didn't show up? *What if Mr. Spencer didn't show up?* After pacing back and forth for another few wasted minutes, Jake decided he couldn't wait any longer. He had to leave if he had any hope of meeting Mr. Spencer on time at the driving range. He didn't know if the golf pro would be there, but he knew he'd never get a chance like this again.

Jake hurried down the shadowy sidewalk as fast as his legs would take him. As he crossed the thirteenth tee, he checked his watch. *Yikes!* He'd have to pick it up if he was going to make it. After a quick hike along the eighteenth fairway he'd be at the clubhouse and then it was just a short chip shot away to the driving range, with its wide fairway and row of tees to hit from. Jake was headed for the very spot where Royal Calgary members would go to practise or get a lesson from one of the club pros.

Jake's face broke into a big grin when he saw the black BMW sitting by itself in the parking lot. Cliff Spencer was already at one of the practice tees, a big wire bucket of golf balls on the grass beside him.

"Morning, Jake!" the golf pro called, giving him a welcoming wave. "Where's Randy?"

"Oh, he couldn't make it, he's … sick," Jake offered.

"That's too bad. I hope he gets better soon."

"So, what club do I hit first, Mr. Spencer?" asked

Jake, eager to start the lesson and to stop talking about Randy.

"First of all, call me Cliff. Everyone else does," Cliff said with a smile. "And second of all, you won't be hitting with a club just yet."

"But I thought I was here to straighten out my duckhook."

"You are and you will. But for the first five minutes we're going to stretch the golf muscles we're going to be using." Jake had read about a full warm-up, but he was always so rushed in the morning he just loosened up a bit by swinging a club.

Cliff demonstrated for Jake the proper stretching technique. He started at the top of his body by turning his neck from side to side, then worked his way down his shoulders, arms, back, and legs. As Cliff performed each stretch, Jake copied him, trying to look like the splitting image of his instructor. Jake thought he was doing a good job with the stretches, but wanted to get going with the real lesson. As soon as every muscle had been stretched and loosened up, he picked up his three-iron and started swinging.

"That's a pretty good swing you have there, but there's only one problem." Cliff was watching Jake closely.

Jake hadn't been swinging for more than ten seconds and Cliff had already found a problem. *Jeez! This can't be good*, thought Jake.

"The problem isn't your swing, but the club you're swinging," Cliff observed. "You want to start off with a high-numbered club that's easy to hit with and that sends the ball high but not too far."

"Like my nine-iron?" Jake asked, looking hopeful.

"Your nine-iron would be perfect." Cliff smiled and took a step back to give Jake more room to swing.

Under Cliff's watchful eye, Jake hit a half dozen nine-iron shots, aiming at a red flag that stood 100 yards out on the range. There were other coloured flags — blue, white, yellow, and black — placed at varied distances as practice targets. Some of Jake's shots flew to the left of the red target, some to the right, and some just a few feet off the ground. Cliff suggested Jake position the ball more toward the middle of his stance. The next few balls he hit soared high into the blue sky and landed softly near the red flagstick. Jake was amazed. All Cliff had to do was study Jake's swing and make a couple of simple suggestions, and suddenly Jake was hitting like a real golfer. Cliff must be the best pro in Alberta — maybe in all of Canada.

"Okay, let's try to pluck the feathers off that duckhook of yours," Cliff said, giving Jake a smile. "What clubs are causing the trouble?"

"Mostly my driver and this one." Jake held up his three-iron.

"Then show me what you've got with the iron."

Jake bent over to place another ball on the tee.

Then he stood up, steadied himself, flexed his knees, and took a big swing. *Thwack!* Sure enough, the ball started off low and straight, but then snapped sharply to the left, diving into the grass not more than 100 yards away. Jake knew that the little white ball wasn't a duck, but he could almost hear it quacking.

Cliff watched Jake hit a few more balls without saying a word. Almost every shot was a duckhook. With every swing Jake got more frustrated and more embarrassed. Finally, Cliff had seen enough.

"Let's take a look at how you're holding the club," Cliff suggested. "I think you may have what we call a strong grip."

Jake gripped the club as he always did, with both hands turned way to the right.

"Just as I thought." Cliff nodded, reaching over to adjust Jake's grip. "Try shifting your hands a bit to the left. That will help you hit the ball straighter. Right now, your clubface is putting a lot of spin on the ball, which is another way of saying — "

"I'll duckhook!" said Jake, finishing Cliff's sentence.

For the next fifteen minutes Jake hit shots, adjusting his grip the way Cliff had shown him. It was like magic. Every ball went straight as an arrow, or almost, with just a small hook. Cliff called the small curve a "draw," and said most of the golfers at Royal Calgary could only dream of having a natural draw to their shots. Jake beamed. He was finally doing something right.

Jake was concentrating so hard on his shots, he hadn't noticed that the time was flying as fast as the balls. When he finally remembered to check the time, he knew he had to hurry back and get ready for his last day of school.

"I guess you'd better be getting back home," Cliff said, seeing the surprise on Jake's face when he looked at his watch. "You know, Jake, I was wondering if you and Randy had any plans for the summer."

"Not really," Jake said. His head was so full of everything he had learned that morning, and the joy of heading off to the last day of school, that he hadn't given a single thought to what the next two months would hold. "We'll probably just golf and go swimming and play video games at Randy's."

"How would you like a summer job?" Cliff asked.

"You're kidding!" Jake's eyes widened with surprise.

"Nope. We need a couple of young, hard-working boys to wash clubs. And I was just wondering if you and Randy would like to spend your summer here on the course. It won't pay much, but — "

"That would be awesome!" Jake cried, jumping in before Cliff could finish his sentence. "But what about our lessons?"

"One week from today, same time, same place."

"All right!" Jake pumped his arm in the air.

"Good, then we have a deal, assuming that Randy wants the job too," Cliff smiled and reached out to shake Jake's hand, "and that it's okay with your parents. Starting Saturday morning, you and Randy will be the newest employees at Royal Calgary."

Wait till he told Randy! Jake felt a twinge in his stomach, but it wasn't that he was hungry for breakfast. Since the lesson began, he hadn't given Randy a second thought. He had been thinking only about his own game the entire time. Maybe he should have waited longer for Randy. Two hours before, Jake didn't trust Randy for being late. Now, Jake wondered if he was the one who couldn't be trusted.

8 Lost and Found

"You should have waited," Randy complained, sitting next to Jake on the bus as it bumped along the road to school for the last time before the summer break.

"I didn't think you were coming!" Jake said.

"My alarm didn't go off and I woke up late," Randy explained. "I'm surprised I even made the bus."

"I thought that maybe you didn't want to come." Jake felt guilty saying it, knowing full well that Randy had been looking forward to the lesson as much as he had.

"Yeah, right!" Randy said, sarcasm clear in his voice. "I wanted to miss this once-in-a-lifetime chance to get a lesson from a real golf pro."

Jake finally gave up trying to wriggle out of the situation and came clean. "I know. I should have waited longer." He looked Randy straight in the eye to show he meant it. "But I have some news that will make up for it."

"It better be good," Randy said, still steamed, but getting curious.

"It is." Jake could barely contain his excitement, and bounced up and down in the bus seat even more than the rough road called for. "Cliff offered both of us jobs for the summer!"

"Doing what?" Randy asked. "I don't think we're quite good enough to be golf pros."

"No, we're not — not yet. But we *are* good enough to wash the members' clubs after they play!"

For the rest of that morning at Evergreen Junior High, Jake, and Randy couldn't stop beaming. All the other students sitting in the gym at the year-end assembly probably thought they were happy because school was ending at noon that day. All the teachers must have thought they were smiling because they had both passed and were being promoted to the next grade. Only Jake and Randy knew the real reason — and they weren't telling.

★   ★   ★

That afternoon, Jake and Randy lazed on the front lawn in the shade of a towering poplar. Another school year was over and there was no better place to be than sitting under a tall tree sipping chilled glasses of ice-cold lemonade. Jake thought he could stay there forever — or at least for the rest of the afternoon.

Five minutes later he was bored.

"Why don't we go look for golf balls?" Jake said, finally thinking of something else to do. "I lost a ton in the woods with all those duckhooks. I've only got a few left and could use some more."

Since Jake couldn't afford new balls, he and Randy always played with ones they found. Whenever their stash got low they would go on a mission looking for balls "Missing In Action." The best place to search for MIA balls was in the woods along the fairways of Royal Calgary. They could usually fill a small bag in only an hour.

Before heading out on Operation Ball Hunt, Jake and Randy changed into their special ball-hunter clothes. They put on brown shorts and green T-shirts so they would blend in with the wooded surroundings of the golf course. They needed to be camouflaged so they wouldn't be seen when they entered enemy territory. The two boys ended up looking like a couple of trees — a couple of trees that walked and talked.

Jake and Randy raced to the end of the street, crossed the field, and hopped over the fence, all as usual. They started their special assignment by looking for balls that had been hooked or sliced deep into the woods. The farther they stayed from the open fairway, the less chance there was of being spotted by the golfers who were playing on the course.

They trudged slowly through the trees, using their built-in ball radar to scan under leaves and bushes as they went. Jake and Randy didn't speak a word. Instead, they signalled to each other by pointing and waving their arms in the direction they were going to take their search.

After a few minutes they had found exactly zero balls. So far, Operation Ball Hunt was a complete failure. The situation called for a change in plans.

"Let's go in the Danger Zone," whispered Randy, pointing to an area closer to the fairway. It was a riskier mission and they had to be careful — the chance of being caught there was much greater. But there was also a much greater chance of finding lost balls. Jake motioned Randy to crouch low, and they crept closer to the short grass of the fifth fairway. The fifth hole was a long par four with a dogleg corner to the left. A lot of golfers misjudged the distance to the bend and accidentally hit their shots too far, and into the waiting woods. It was a gold mine for balls.

Just as they predicted, Jake and Randy discovered balls everywhere in the Danger Zone — beside high evergreens, under low bushes, and between gnarled roots. They started to fill their bags as if they were on an Easter-egg hunt. Soon, both hunters had captured their share of white, dimpled loot. Jake decided the operation was a success and waved to Randy, signalling they could return to headquarters.

Whoooosh! Suddenly, a ball came flying into the woods.

"Incoming!" yelled Randy, breaking their code of silence.

The ball landed just about a yard from where Jake and Randy were hiding. "That was a close one!" Jake was still covering his head with his hands.

"Hey, look at this!" Randy kneeled down to more closely inspect the white missile. "The ball has the letters *TJD* marked on it."

"TJD … TJD … TJD … " Jake repeated slowly. Randy looked at Jake. Jake looked at Randy.

"TJ Davis!" they shrieked together.

When the two boys peered through the leaves out into the fairway, there was TJ, marching straight toward them, with Brandon, Ryan, and Zach not far behind. If the Fearsome Foursome found Jake and Randy collecting lost balls — *their* lost balls — Jake and Randy were going to fast become the Terminated Twosome!

Randy grabbed the ball and the two boys took off, darting from tree-to-tree before diving behind a thick clump of bushes. They lay completely still, barely daring to even take a breath.

"I was sure my ball came into the woods about here," they heard TJ say. They also heard the rustle as he brushed the leaves back with his hands, and the dragging sound of his feet as he started trudging through the trees. "You guys, spread out and start looking."

Thump ... thump ... thump! What was loudest to Jake was his heart beating inside his chest like a scared rabbit. Every second that ticked by seemed to take a whole minute.

"We can't look too long." That was Brandon's voice. "The group playing right behind us will get mad."

"I guess you're right," TJ said. "I was positive we'd find my ball right here. It's kind of a mystery how it disappeared. Let's go."

As the Fearsome Foursome tramped through the woods, back out onto the fifth fairway, Jake and Randy could finally stop holding their breaths. *Whew!* They slowly got to their knees, but stayed crouched behind the bush until it was safe to stand up.

"Yup, it's a real mystery how that ball disappeared," Randy smiled, clutching TJ's ball in his hand.

"Mission accomplished," Jake said. "Time to head back to the base." Jake didn't feel cheap for taking TJ's ball after his bad shot. After all, TJ was always taking cheap shots at him.

9 Under Attack

At exactly seven-fifty-five that Saturday morning, Jake did something he had never done before. He walked along the private road that led to the Royal Calgary Golf Club, out in broad daylight where anybody could see him. Three hours earlier, he and Randy had sneaked onto the course to play their usual four holes, but now they were on their way to becoming official Royal Calgary employees. They were finally allowed to enter the exclusive club the same way all the members did — through the front gate.

Lining both sides of the winding road were tall poplar trees, standing at attention like soldiers guarding the entrance. Now that he wasn't running full-speed by the clubhouse, Jake could study it more closely. The building was a lot bigger and older than he remembered. He could see a shiny metal plaque hanging over the front doorway with the date 1922 engraved on it. *That's even older than my grandpa,* Jake thought to himself.

The clubhouse stood two storeys high and was built of large grey stones and dark-brown wooden planks. It reminded Jake of an old English castle. All that was missing was a drawbridge and a deep moat with crocodiles swimming in the water.

Jake and Randy stood in front of the clubhouse, trying to figure out where they would find Cliff.

"Let's go in the Members Only entrance," Jake said. They had climbed halfway up the steps toward the shiny gold door when Jake noticed a wooden sign with an arrow: "PRO SHOP THIS WAY."

A paved path led the boys down a small hill and around the back of the clubhouse. Two rows of white golf carts were lined up on the pavement, waiting for the members to drive to the first hole and start playing their rounds. Jake and Randy walked by the carts and into the Pro Shop.

"Hey, guys!" welcomed Cliff, who was standing behind the counter near the entrance. "Right on time."

"Wow!" cried Jake and Randy together.

Jake had never seen so much golf equipment! Callaway, Cleveland, Nike, Ping, TaylorMade — every brand of club he had ever heard of was right there in front of him. There were putters of all shapes and sizes lined up against one wall, and shelves of shirts, sweaters, jackets, and shoes on another. Right in the middle of the floor was a huge selection of brightly coloured bags. Jake's eyes were as big as golf balls.

"There will be plenty of time later on to check out all the equipment." Cliff laughed at how wide-eyed the two boys were. "But Saturday is our busiest day at the Club, so let's get to work."

The boys followed Cliff out of the Pro Shop and into the bright sunlight before walking into the small building next door. It seemed dark inside at first, but once Jake's eyes adjusted to the dim light he could see long rows of golf bags. Each bag sat in its own wooden stall and had a white tag over it with a member's name and a number.

Cliff took his time explaining to the boys how their summer job would work. When Royal Calgary members arrived at the course, Jake and Randy would take their names and find the right bags. Then they would carry them out, and strap them to the back of a power cart if the members were driving the course, or stand them on the ground if the players were walking. When members had finished playing their round, the boys would take the bags over to the wash area. There, they would clean the clubs with the "high-tech cleaning device" otherwise known as a brush and a bucket of soapy water. After the clubs were shiny again, the bags would be returned to the members' stalls, ready for the next game. That was it.

"Now for the most important part of the job," Cliff said, smiling. "You get paid every two weeks."

Paid? Jake had forgotten all about the money. He had been so stoked to actually be allowed on Royal Calgary, he hadn't even thought about the money he would earn.

I'm going to save up enough to buy a new nine-iron. Or a three-iron … he daydreamed. He wasn't sure what he would get first. He needed pretty much everything.

Jake bounded into action. For the next few hours he fetched clubs: "Coming right up, Mr. Flynn." He cleaned clubs: "We'll have these blades looking like new, Mrs. Hutton." And he put clubs away: "They'll be ready for your game tomorrow, Mr. Lester." The members appreciated the boys' hard work. One of them even gave Jake a toonie tip just for getting his clubs, something he was supposed to do anyway!

Cliff came by to see how they were doing, and told the boys to keep up the good work. Even though he had never had a summer job before, Jake couldn't imagine there being a better one.

That is, until he was alone in the bag room and outside someone began yelling, "I need some help here. Someone get my clubs!"

Jake's throat went dry. He recognized the voice. It was TJ.

"What are you doing here, Junkyard?" TJ asked snidely as he entered the room. He walked right up to

Jake and stood in front of him.

"I work here," Jake said, looking him in the eye.

"Is that right? Well, I guess someone has to fetch and clean my clubs, and it might as well be you."

Jake kept his mouth clamped shut. He knew he had a job to do, so he asked for TJ's number, then disappeared to retrieve his clubs. He walked along the stalls until he came to *TJ Davis: #182*. Jake couldn't help but stare at TJ's brand new set of clubs, gleaming even in the dim light. Jake had seen the X-Series irons featured in the latest golf magazines and had dreamed of one day owning them.

"Nice clubs," Jake said as he handed TJ his bag.

"Yeah, they're okay, I guess. But they're not helping my game much," TJ complained. "I'm thinking about getting a new set."

When TJ was joined by Brandon, Ryan, and Zach, all members of the Fearsome Foursome were present and accounted for. As usual, they all wore the same uniform — today it was red hats, white shirts, and navy blue pants. Jake was outnumbered. He looked around anxiously for Randy, but didn't see him.

"Don't worry, bag boy," Zach said, laughing. "Your little bag buddy is off getting our clubs."

Sure enough, Randy came trudging out of the bag room loaded down with not just one big bag, but all three. With a mighty heave, he stood them up in front of Brandon, Ryan, and Zach. The Fearsome

Foursome picked up their bags and started walking to the first tee to start their round.

"See ya, losers!" TJ called over his shoulder.

"You're the only loser here," Jake muttered under his breath.

"What was that, Junkyard?" said TJ, whipping around. "Did you say something?"

"No," Jake lied.

"Yes, you did." TJ marched over to Jake and pushed him down to the ground.

"Hey, watch it!" cried Randy, seeing a trickle of blood ooze from a cut on Jake's arm.

"That's enough!" yelled a voice from the doorway of the Pro Shop. "Break it up!" In just a few seconds Cliff's large frame was standing between the two much smaller fighters.

"He started it!" said TJ, pointing at Jake.

"No, you started it!" said Jake as he picked himself up off the ground.

"I don't care who started it," said Cliff. "But I know who's going to end it — me. If I ever catch either one of you fighting again, I'll send both of you home. And neither of you will be playing or working here for a long, long time. Got it?"

TJ and Jake both nodded their heads. Cliff gave them each one more stern look and waited until the Fearsome Foursome left.

Jake felt embarrassed. He couldn't believe that

Cliff had seen TJ pick on him. But then Jake felt something else replace the embarrassment when he realized that, for once, he had talked back and stood up for himself.

10 Like a Rocket

As the sun-baked days of July passed, Jake could feel himself getting stronger and stronger. His arms and legs gained muscle from carrying the heavy golf bags and his hands became more powerful from cleaning clubs. It was hard work, but it was paying off in more ways than one. Jake's golf game was improving, and his savings account was bulking up along with his muscles.

He didn't even feel he was missing his summer break, because he didn't work every day. Cliff said not as many members played at the beginning of the week, so Jake had every Monday and Tuesday off. And since Cliff wasn't as busy on those days, that was when he continued giving Jake and Randy their early-morning lessons. Of all the great things about that July, those lessons were the highlight for Jake.

Usually Cliff taught both boys, but when Randy was away on a week-long vacation to Victoria with his family, Jake had a lesson all to himself. *Sometimes there are advantages to not going on fancy vacations*, he thought.

When Jake arrived at the range, he saw Cliff already out practising with a big bucket of balls. He was deep in concentration, hitting towering shots out toward the blue flagsticks on the fairway. Jake waited until Cliff finished his last shot.

"What club are we going to learn today?" he asked. In previous lessons Cliff had shown them the proper technique for hitting short irons, like the eight-iron, nine-iron, and wedge, and for hitting long irons, such as the three-, four-, and five-irons.

"We're going to hit the big sticks — the woods and the driver." He never called them metals, even though that's what they were all made of now. "Way back in the last century, when I learned to play as a boy, they were called woods," he explained.

Jake owned an old driver that really was made of wood. He usually left it at home, thinking it was better to learn how to hit his irons properly. When he had decided three clubs were all he could carry for his early-morning secret missions, he had chosen the three- and nine-irons, plus his putter.

Cliff taught Jake how to hit his small driver, then handed him his own driver. Jake couldn't believe how massive it was. The head was the size of a grapefruit — maybe even a melon! But it was so light he wondered how it could launch a ball so far. When Cliff hit his driver, the ball took off like it was shot out of a cannon and rocketed so far away it almost disappeared from view. It was a white speck against the blue sky.

When Jake swung Cliff's driver the ball took off — maybe not like a rocket, but at least like a fighter jet. There was a loud *Piiing!* when the ball made contact with the metal face of the club, and it flew more than 200 yards down the practice range. Jake had never hit a ball that far before. It occurred to him that maybe he should be saving his money for a big driver like Cliff's.

Finally, Cliff told Jake there was only one more club left to learn — the flatstick.

Jake thought he knew the name of every club there was, but he hadn't heard of that one. Was it some kind of special club only used by pros? "The flat-what?" he asked, looking confused.

"Flatstick is another name for your putter," Cliff explained. "Instead of learning about it here on the practice range, we're going to walk over there." He pointed to a putting green dotted with nine small red flags, one for each hole.

Jake followed Cliff over to the practice putting green. When the boys played in the early morning, they never spent too long lining up their putts. They had to keep moving to play as many holes as they could in as little time as possible. Studying the breaks of every putt would have slowed them down. Jake had the feeling that his attitude to putting was about to change.

"Putting is over 40 percent of golf," Cliff explained. "So, if you shoot 100 … "

"You take at least forty putts," Jake said, finishing the formula.

"And that's a lot of shots. So it's important to practise your putting."

Jake had never thought about it that way.

"Judging whether a putt will break to the left or right is important," Cliff continued, "but so is speed. Your ball will roll slow or fast depending on how short the grass is cut, and whether you are putting uphill or down."

Jake couldn't wait to show Cliff how well he could knock the ball into the cup with his flatstick. But before he could make a single putt, he watched Cliff pace off 30 feet nowhere near the hole, then reach into his pocket for a long white tee, and stick it into the grass.

"Isn't golf about putting the ball into the hole?" asked Jake.

"It sure is," said Cliff. "But first we're going to try aiming at a smaller target."

For the next fifteen minutes Jake putted at the slender tee from different parts of the green. His speed control got better with almost every putt so that, by the end, his balls were coming to rest within a foot of his target. Once or twice a putt even hit the tee.

Next, Cliff told Jake to putt from only 10 feet

away. His strokes were slow and smooth, and the putts hit the tee more times than they missed.

"Now, it's time to putt at a real hole," Cliff announced, pulling the tee from the green and pointing to the first hole with the short red flagstick. "Wait until you see what happens."

"Wow! The hole seems gigantic," Jake cried, watching his first ball roll straight into the cup. "I feel like I can't miss!"

"Pretty good trick, eh?" Cliff said. "The cup looks as big as a bucket compared to the tee, doesn't it? You feel more confident, and confidence is a big part of putting well. One of the most important things to do in golf, Jake, is be confident."

As the sun continued to rise, Jake continued to putt. He played all nine holes on the practice green. Not every putt plunked into the bottom of the cup, but even the ones that missed rolled only a few inches past. Jake had never putted so well.

Jake enjoyed talking to Cliff during his lessons and wished there was some way to make the conversations last longer. "Do you want to come over for dinner tonight, Cliff?" Jake blurted out as he picked up his clubs. He had meant to ask weeks ago, but had been too nervous. Plus, what if Cliff said something to his mom about TJ pushing him? Jake had been wearing long sleeves to cover the cut on his arm, and his mom had been too busy to notice.

Still, his mom kept saying that she wanted to meet Cliff, since Jake was spending so much time with him. Dinner would be the perfect opportunity for his mom to see that Cliff wasn't the ogre she thought he was.

"That's a friendly offer," Cliff replied to the invitation. "But I'm sure your Mother is busy and doesn't need an unexpected guest showing up."

"Oh, it was her idea!" Jake said quickly. "She wants to meet you. She says she has some questions for you, that kind of stuff."

"Well, if it's okay with your Mother, then I'd be happy to accept."

"Great! We usually have dinner at about six o'clock."

"Then I'll see you at six."

11 Guess Who's Coming for Dinner?

"You asked Mr. Spencer *what?*" Jake's mom shrieked. "You're kidding, right?"

"Nope, he'll be here for dinner in an hour," Jake said. "But don't worry, Mom, he's a really nice guy. He won't even mind if you look the way you do now. And he mostly eats in greasy fast-food restaurants, so I'm sure your cooking will be good enough for him."

"Gee, thanks for the compliments." Finally she was smiling. "I'm glad I'll finally get to meet him, Jake, but I never asked you to invite him over for dinner. And I would have liked a little more notice … "

"Please!" Jake pleaded.

Over the next hour, Jake watched his mom spring into action. First, she disappeared into the bathroom, saying she wanted to make herself "presentable." A few minutes later the door opened and she came out looking … pretty much the same, at least to Jake. She then walked through the living room, straightening the pillows on the green corduroy couch and picking up scattered newspapers and magazines as she went.

Jake stood back as his mom flung open the doors of the cupboards and fridge, quickly grabbing all the ingredients for macaroni and cheese. Soon, the noodles were in boiling water and the cheese sauce was bubbling away. As she reached into the crisper for lettuce, she called over her shoulder for Jake to set the table.

Ping-dong! The front doorbell rang. The bell was broken, and the first tone was more like a high-pitched *ping* than a *ding*. Jake raced to the door. Through the big picture window he could see Cliff's black BMW parked in the driveway. He swung open the door as his mom suddenly appeared just a few steps behind him, her arms crossed.

"Come on in, Cliff," Jake said excitedly. "This is my mom. She lives here too."

"She does?" Cliff smiled at Jake's mom and pulled two small boxes out of his pocket and handed one to Jake. "These are for you."

"Three new golf balls!" said Jake excitedly.

"And I didn't want to forget the hostess, so I brought you some too, Mrs. Cooper." Cliff gave Jake's mom the other box. Jake's mom snickered and put them down on the hall table. Jake was pretty sure she'd never been given golf balls before.

"I really appreciate you inviting me for dinner," Cliff said. "This will be my first home-cooked meal in a long time."

"We've been looking forward to it for a while, Mr. Spencer," Jake's mom said politely, and it was Jake's turn to snicker. As Cliff insisted that Jake's mom call him Cliff, she offered Cliff a seat in the big red armchair. Then she disappeared into the kitchen where dinner was still cooking, and came out carrying three ice-cube-filled glasses of pop. For the next few minutes, Jake talked with Cliff about whether Tiger Woods would win the next golf tournament while his mom zipped back and forth between the two rooms.

"Dinner's on the table!" Jake's mom called from the kitchen.

Jake and Cliff walked in from the living room and sat down at the kitchen table. In front of each of them sat a heaping plateful of golden brown noodles topped with baked cheese. Jake's mom was tossing dressing into the salad greens and piling the salad into three bowls.

Jake's mom apologized for the simple meal. "I arrived home a little later than planned," she said.

"I haven't cooked much for myself in the last couple of years," said Cliff as he took a big forkful of macaroni.

"Two years is a long time," said Jake's mom.

"Yes, it is," he replied. "That's when my wife left."

Jake saw a sympathetic look cross his mom's face. Jake just chewed and chewed in silence.

"The hardest part was watching her take our boy with her to live back in Toronto," Cliff continued. "I don't get to see him very much."

"How old is he?" asked Jake's mom.

"Kyle is twelve, about the same age as Jake now." This time the conversation really did stop short.

"There has been one advantage to eating at fast-food restaurants, though," Cliff said after a few moments, changing to a happier subject. "There haven't been any dishes to wash afterward!"

Jake knew that wasn't going to be the case that night — it was his job to do the dishes, and macaroni was always impossible to scrape out of the pot if he left it for too long.

"Why don't we go sit in the living room while Jake cleans up, Cliff," said Jake's mom. "There are some things I want to talk to you about."

They all got up from the table. As Jake started to pile the dirty dishes in the sink, he listened for the conversation in the next room.

Jake's mom got right to it. "Sorry if I'm being too blunt, Cliff, but I'm not quite sure why you're giving free lessons to my son. It's a very admirable thing to do, but frankly, it strikes me as a little odd."

"Well, there are three reasons," Cliff replied. "The most important one is that he has talent — a lot of talent. Jake has the best natural swing of any junior golfer I've ever taught."

Jake just about dropped a plate on the floor! He didn't want his mom and Cliff to know he was listening, so he turned on the tap and started to fill the sink with water. So Cliff really thought he was a good golfer, or at least had the potential to become one! He felt a warm glow that had nothing to do with the hot water running over his hands.

"Yes, Jake's good at everything he does," said his mom. "What about the second?"

"It's a real pleasure to teach boys like Jake and Randy. They really want to learn, unlike some of the kids at Royal Calgary, who think they know it all and don't even listen."

"And the last reason?"

"I probably don't have to tell you that Jake reminds me of my own boy," said Cliff slowly. "I like to think that whatever my son was interested in, someone would be there for him to learn from and trust."

Jake's mom fell silent. Jake finished putting away the dishes and stuck his head around the corner to see if Cliff was still there or if his mom had eaten him.

"Come on in, Jake. We were just talking about you." His mom pointed at the shabby green couch. "I was just thanking Cliff for giving you lessons. There still is something that I'm worried about, though."

"What's that?" asked Cliff, sounding concerned.

"Jake practises too much," she said, eyeing her son. "He doesn't sleep enough. He just pushes himself too hard."

Jake expected Cliff to take his side, and was sure that he would say the only way to play better was to do all three of those things.

"Your Mom's right, Jake," Cliff said, nodding his head. "If you're not careful, you'll burn out. You don't have to practise every single day. I don't. Some mornings you should sleep in and just spend the day hanging out with Randy."

Jake could see his mom raise her eyebrows and smile, just as surprised as Jake that Cliff was agreeing with her.

12 Sign Here

The day Randy came home from his holiday, he and Jake went in to work early to visit the Pro Shop and check out the new stock. They couldn't afford most of the expensive clubs, but they could always dream. They walked down the entrance hall of the club, staring up at the photographs that hung on the dark wood walls all the way to the shop. Nicklaus ... Palmer ... Trevino ... just some of the big-name golfers who had played the course throughout its long and famous history. Jake wondered if Cliff had ever played with any of the old masters.

At the Pro shop, Randy and Jake drooled over the shiny new golf clubs. Jake wondered what it would be like to have a complete set of matching irons, instead of the old collection of totally different clubs he had. The money in his bank account was growing, but it would still take a long time until he could afford pricey clubs like these.

"Hi, boys!" Jake and Randy turned to see Cliff standing by the bulletin board. "Notice anything new posted up here?"

Jake and Randy had walked past the bulletin board a hundred times without ever paying it much attention. After all, the announcements tacked on it were "for members only." Curious, they stood right in front of the board, looking straight up at a big green poster.

"Did you read this?" Cliff asked.

"Junior … Club … Championship," Jake read, not really caring.

"What does that have to do with us?" Randy asked.

"Keep reading," Cliff suggested.

Jake continued, " … The Junior Club Championship is open to all members *and* employees of Royal Calgary." Jake thought for a couple of seconds before blurting out, "And we're employees!"

"Why don't you two sign up?" Cliff pointed to the small pencil on the wooden ledge at the bottom of the board. Jake wasn't sure he and Randy should enter. Neither of them had ever played golf against anyone but each other. But if Cliff thought they were good enough, then maybe they should give it a shot.

Jake picked up the pencil and printed his name on the dotted line, then passed the pencil to Randy so he could do the same. Jake and Randy were the first junior players to sign the list. But Jake knew they wouldn't be the last.

"Now, boys, I need someone to fill in for Jordan today. He drives the range cart and picks up all the balls on the driving range, but he called in sick. The members won't be pleased if we run out of range balls. Could I get one of you to take Jordan's place?"

Jake wanted to drive the range cart, but he could tell that Randy did as well. "Go for it, man," said Randy. "I just got back from Victoria, and I bet you've been spending all your time in the bag room."

"Since you're both going to be extra busy today, I'll double your regular pay," Cliff said. The boys eagerly nodded in agreement. It was decided. Randy went back to cleaning clubs and Jake hurried over to the practice range.

It didn't take Jake long to get the hang of driving the range cart. It was just like a regular golf cart, but a little bigger. The cart was white with one fat rubber wheel in front and two behind. A small trailer was hooked to the back, where the yellow range balls were fed after automatically being picked up below. A strong metal cage shielded Jake from any balls that might accidentally be hit near him.

For the first couple of hours Jake criss-crossed the range, making sure he didn't miss any of the bright yellow balls that blanketed the grass. The range had twenty individual practice stalls at one end. Each stall had a big green mat made of artificial turf and a rubber tee from which players hit. Jake managed to fill the trailer twice and returned the loads to the big metal ball dispenser that looked like an over-sized pop machine. The only difference was that, instead of cans of Coke, balls came out the bottom. The day was going so smoothly that Jake began to relax.

He shouldn't have.

Jake looked from the far end of the range to see that a group of four golfers had just arrived. Jake could see them gather around the big green machine, collecting buckets of balls. When their wire buckets were full, the golfers took their clubs and each marched over to a practice stall. As Jake drove closer, he realized they weren't just any golfers. It was the Fearsome Foursome. His heart started to beat faster as he could clearly see TJ, Brandon, Ryan, and Zach. The boys stood lined up at four stalls in a row, and they were all pointing straight at Jake!

"Looks like we've got ourselves a little target practice!" Jake heard TJ shout to his friends.

"And the target is our competition!" yelled Ryan.

"I can't believe he signed up for the Club Championship," screamed Zach.

"He's got a lot of nerve showing his name around here!" called Brandon.

"And his face!" TJ laughed.

Jake realized he was in trouble, but he didn't see

any way out. He had a job to do. He gritted his teeth and continued driving the cart back and forth, just 150 yards in front of the firing squad.

At exactly the same time, each of the Fearsome Foursome pulled a shiny five-iron from his bag. The metal clubs gleamed like swords in the sunlight. Next, they each bent over and placed a ball on their tee. Then all four got ready to hit, taking dead aim at their target. Jake watched helplessly from his cage as they loaded up in unison. It was like being in a duck shooting gallery at the arcade — and every duck wore Jake's face.

"Ready ... aim ... fire!" shouted TJ.

Zing! Zing! Zing! The first three balls shot out like bullets. But Jake was lucky — each ball zoomed by the cart, narrowly missing him. Jake was hoping that maybe he would escape when ... *Clang!* The fourth ball was a direct hit. It ricocheted off the metal cage close to Jake's head and bounced harmlessly away on the grass. Jake's heart was pounding. He took a deep breath to calm down and tried to keep his hands steady on the steering wheel. He sneaked a quick look at the Fearsome Foursome and could see them high-fiving each other for the one successful hit.

It wouldn't be long before Jake could turn the cart around and head the other way. In another minute he would be out of range. One ... two ... three ... the seconds took forever to click by. *Zing! Clang! Zing!*

Clang! A second round of yellow missiles was launched at the cart — two of them jangled the cage and jolted Jake. He stepped on the gas pedal as hard as he could, but it made no difference. The range cart had only one speed — slow. Jake crawled along like a helpless turtle.

Zing! Zing! Zing! Zing! This time all four balls whistled by the cart, landing on the grass and bounding away. He must be getting out of range. Jake took another quick glance over his shoulder. He saw that the Fearsome Foursome had stopped their target practice now that he was out of reach. TJ, Brandon, Ryan, and Zach picked up their bags and started to walk back toward the clubhouse.

"We'll see you on the first tee of the Club Championship," TJ turned to yell back at Jake.

"Yeah, if you even know where that is!" shrieked Zach, causing TJ, Brandon, and Ryan to crack up with laughter.

Jake stopped the cart, wiped the beads of sweat from his brow, and breathed a huge sigh of relief. While he was glad that he managed to avoid a confrontation with TJ, he was getting fed up with all of his teasing, and was ready for things to change. The Fearsome Foursome may have won this battle, but Jake still had a chance to win the golf war.

13 Let Down

Just seven early morning missions. That's all Jake and Randy had to get their games into top form so they could compete against the Fearsome Foursome in the Junior Club Championship. They were relying on Cliff to give them some pro tips during their final lesson together but, as it turned out, they were on their own.

"I'm afraid I can't make Tuesday morning, boys," Cliff announced to Jake and Randy. "I've just got too many members asking me for lessons. The tournament for the adults is held on the same day, so there are a lot of extra requests. Everybody wants last minute tune-ups to improve their swings and their scores."

As Cliff walked away, Jake turned to Randy. "What about us? Aren't we important? Maybe Cliff really cares only about teaching the members who can throw money around."

"This does suck," replied Randy evenly. "But we'll still be able to practise. We'll be fine."

"Yeah, forget Cliff." Jake turned away from Randy, trying to hide how hurt he was. "We'll just train by ourselves, right?"

"Right," said Randy.

★   ★   ★

That night, the boys sat in Jake's kitchen and plotted out a strategy. They would practise one part of their game on each of the next seven days. Jake remembered seeing a chart in *How to Golf Like a Pro*. TJ may have taken the book, but Jake had every page memorized and intact in his head. He wrote down the practice timetable on a piece of paper and stuck it to the fridge with a white magnet shaped like a golf ball.

Following the list, Jake and Randy would start with putting, then work their way down to the longer

Saturday:	Putting
Sunday:	Sand traps
Monday:	Chipping
Tuesday:	Wedges
Wednesday:	Short irons
Thursday:	Long irons
Friday:	Driving

shots. By Friday they would be hitting their drivers, perfectly preparing them for Saturday's tee-off on the first hole of the Club Championship. They had a plan, and as long as they stuck to it, they would play better than they ever had before.

The next morning, Jake and Randy walked onto the thirteenth green just after dawn to practise their putting. Jake stuck a tee in the green and paced off 30 feet, just like Cliff had taught him. For the next half-hour the boys putted at the tee from points on a big circle around the target. Each ball left a long trail through the thick dew, marking how the putts were rolling on the green. As the sun started climbing higher in the sky, Jake and Randy moved in closer to practise their shorter putts.

A few minutes before they returned home, Jake pulled out the tee. He was ready to start putting at the real hole.

"The hole seems huge!" Jake cried, watching his ball disappear into the cup.

"It's not a cup, it's a bucket," Randy laughed, sinking a long curving putt of his own.

Their first practice had gone exactly as planned. Jake felt something rise in him. He was no longer upset that Cliff wouldn't be giving them their final lesson. For the first time, Jake felt like he could do this — he deserved to play well in the Championship, and maybe even win.

Jake wanted the week to fly by, but the time seemed to move like a ball stuck in the long grass of the deep rough. Jake had collected all his mismatched clubs and put them in his old tattered golf bag. They may not have been the best clubs, or all the same, but at least he had a complete set. Jake knew he would need every last one for the Championship.

By Wednesday morning, they were practising their short iron shots. Jake carried the seven-, eight-, and nine-irons in his hand, and some extra golf balls in his pocket as they arrived at the thirteenth hole. Jake and Randy walked along the fairway to a position 100 yards from the green, marked by red stakes placed in the ground on both sides of the fairway. The white markers showed a distance 150 yards from the green. The markers helped golfers choose a club to accurately reach the flag on each hole.

Jake tossed five of his balls on the grass. Randy moved a few steps to the right and emptied his pockets. The boys hit the balls one by one using their eight-irons. Every ball sailed over the green and fell about 10 yards on the other side! Randy looked at Jake, his confusion showing all over his face.

"Don't worry," Jake reassured his friend. "We didn't hit the right club. That's why we're practising. Let's try our nine-irons. The shots shouldn't go as far."

The boys ran to pick up their balls and hoofed it back along the fairway to the red 100-yard marker.

They lined up their balls on the grass and tried again.

"That's more like it!" Jake watched his first shot land softly on the front of the green, then roll toward the flag in the middle of the putting surface.

Both boys hit their next four shots with similar results. Not every ball landed on the green, but even the ones that missed flew the right distance.

"Mark it down," Randy said. "At 100 yards, we use our nine-irons."

Jake pulled a small green pencil and a piece of paper out of his pocket. He wrote *100–9*. He'd remember what that stood for later. He smiled at the numbers, thinking that their secret missions now had a secret code.

The boys continued practising their short irons, moving back about 10 yards for each change in club. That meant when they were 110 yards away from the green, they would hit their eight-irons, and when their balls were 120 yards from the flagstick, they would hit their seven-irons. Jake wrote down *110–8, 120–7*. By the end of the week they would have a handy list of how far they could hit every club.

Suddenly, Jake and Randy realized how much time had passed, and scrambled. They had to hightail it to the other Club — the Club where they still had a full day's work ahead of them.

14 Tough Break

Finally, it was Friday — the day before the Championship. It was the last morning to practise and Jake and Randy were down to the final club, the driver. Jake had a driver in his bag, but it wasn't new, it wasn't made of metal, and it wasn't as big as a grapefruit, like Cliff's. It was old, made of wood, and had a head about the size of an orange. Still, he would depend on the old club for a good start on the longer holes at Royal Calgary. Without it, Jake wouldn't stand a chance against the new drivers played by the Fearsome Foursome.

There were banks of low, grey clouds hanging over the thirteenth fairway. Jake didn't know why, but he felt as gloomy as the day. He and Randy stood on the tee, swinging two clubs each to help them warm up. After several smooth practice swings, they were ready to hit a few drives for real. Jake was still trying to prevent his drives from spinning wildly into the left rough. He'd be happy if he never saw another duckhook for the rest of his life. He teed up his first ball and stood over it, checked his grip, then swung. The ball took off like it was launched from a slingshot, zooming straight down the fairway.

"Sweet. Now *that's* what I like to see," Jake said, feeling his spirits start to lift. "A few more like that and I'll be ready for tomorrow."

Jake and Randy hit five drives each, every ball coming to a stop almost 200 yards away.

Randy started to walk off the tee, heading out to pick up their balls.

"Wait a minute." Jake pulled one last ball from his pocket. "I brought an extra one."

Jake teed up his sixth ball and swung hard. He expected to see his ball sailing down the middle of the fairway. He saw a round object rocketing straight down the fairway, but it flew only about 15 yards, and it wasn't white. It took him a second or two to realize that what he was watching was the black head of his old wooden driver, somersaulting through the air! Jake froze. His eyes stared straight ahead and his mouth locked wide open without a single sound coming out. He saw the look on Randy's face change from confusion to shock.

"Now what am I going to do?" Jake finally said, still holding the headless shaft of his driver. "Without my driver, I'm done."

"I would lend you mine, but I'll sort of be needing it tomorrow." Leave it to Randy to make a small joke, trying to cheer up Jake in the face of disaster.

Jake collected his clubs, or what was left of them, and slowly trudged home. How was he going to beat TJ without a driver? He had no chance!

★ ★ ★

All that day, Jake just wasn't himself at work. He couldn't spring into action whenever he saw a member arrive. His feet dragged when he had to fetch bags, and it seemed to take him an hour just to clean one set of clubs. He was in slow motion.

"You look lower than a snake's belly," Cliff said when he saw Jake moping around. "I thought you'd be excited. Tomorrow's the Championship, you know."

"I know, but I broke my wooden driver this morning! The head just snapped right off."

"That's a tough break." Cliff turned over an empty wash bucket and sat down beside Jake. "Sometimes things look darkest before the dawn."

"Yeah, it was pretty dark this morning," Jake said gloomily, thinking back to standing with Randy on the thirteenth tee at dawn.

"What I mean is, sometimes things seem worse just before they get better," Cliff explained. He sat there quietly, thinking for a few seconds then turning to Jake. "Follow me, I have an idea."

As Cliff led him back into the small building

where the clubs were stored, Jake kept his head down. He was still a little upset with Cliff for not being there to give him a lesson just when he needed it most.

It was grey and quiet in the bag room. There were only a couple of small windows letting in faint rays of streaming light. Jake stood with Cliff inside the door while their eyes adjusted to the darkness. Cliff started walking slowly along the rows of bags, his eyes scanning the names marked over them. After a couple of minutes of searching he reached the end of the last row in the most dimly lit corner. Suddenly, he stopped.

"There it is," Cliff said softly.

Jake had been in the crowded bag room hundreds of times before, but he had never noticed this stall, with this name. Above a large, dusty golf bag the initials *C.S.* were engraved on a special metal tag. *C.S.*, thought Jake, *Cliff Spencer.*

"I put these clubs here a long time ago." Cliff stared at the bag and spoke as if his mind was far away. "They were my clubs when I first turned pro twenty years ago. They were top-of-the-line way back then."

Jake studied the bag. It was made of heavy, black leather and was faded from hundreds of rounds played in the sun, wind, and rain. Popping out of the top of the bag were the heads of a set of irons and a set of woods. The irons were pitted with small nicks and dents, but they had been well cared for. Jake could just imagine all the great shots Cliff must have played with them. Then he noticed a group of three woods, each with its own black leather head cover. One of the woods had a longer shaft and had a head that was much bigger than the others. *That must be the driver,* Jake said to himself.

"There's no sense leaving all these clubs to just collect dust." Cliff reached into the bag and pulled out the biggest one. He handed it to Jake. "This was my favourite club. And I want you to have it, Jake."

"You trust me with your driver?" Jake carefully took off the cover to reveal a large gold-headed club made of metal.

"I can't think of anyone I would trust more."

As Jake followed Cliff out of the dark room, he knew he had to do something he had been thinking about for a long time. When he passed TJ's bag, Jake pulled TJ's "lost" ball from his pocket and returned it to where it belonged.

15 Toss and Turn

"I've got a surprise for you," called Jake's mom as she walked in the front door after work on Friday night.

Jake came running. "What's in there?"

"It's a new golf shirt," she said proudly, handing him the bag. "You deserve to look like the professional that you are."

Jake had decided that he would take Cliff's advice to get more rest, so he thanked his mom, took the shirt and headed down the hall to his bedroom earlier than usual. He knew he needed a good sleep to be ready for the Championship the next morning. But he also knew that it would be hard to sleep at all, when all he could think about was the game.

On the desk where Jake did his homework sat a big, lumpy bag filled with all the balls he had found during his Ball Hunter Operations with Randy that summer. Jake took out the six almost-new balls that Cliff had given him and his mom and inspected each one for cuts in the hard surfaces. These were the ones he would use for his round the next day. Next to the balls he stacked a small pile of white tees. In case he needed to mark the position of his ball on the green, Jake decided to use a gold-coloured souvenir coin his dad had given him the last time they went to the Calgary Stampede together. The final item Jake lined up on his desk was the faded blue cap he had worn for every one of his morning missions. It was a little tattered, but it had brought him good luck in the past. It had to again for at least one more day.

Everything was ready. It was time for sleep. But sleep was the last thing on Jake's mind. Jake wondered how the pros could possibly relax the night before a big tournament. From the moment he climbed under the covers and turned out the light, all Jake did was worry about playing well the next morning. He lay in the darkness with his eyes wide open. He would toss one way. Then turn the other. Finally, he managed to drift off to a sleep that was anything but restful.

Jake dreamed his drive on the first hole duckhooked crazily into the trees on the left … then he woke up. He dreamed it took him ten putts to sink his ball on the second hole … then he woke up. He dreamed there wasn't even a hole to putt into on the third green … then he woke up. And so it went. By the time he had finished playing all eighteen disastrous holes in his dream, Jake had taken 222 shots and finished in last place. The final image of his golfing *frightmare* was of TJ, Brandon, Ryan, and Zach watching him trying to sink his ball on the eighteenth green, and laughing so hard they fell down.

When his alarm started buzzing at seven o'clock the next morning, Jake felt like he hadn't slept at all. He didn't think he had the energy to drag himself out of bed, let alone play the best round of his life. And that was the worst nightmare of all.

16 Zigzag

Jake sat slumped over the kitchen table like a sack of potatoes. His eyes were shut tight. His arms hung limply at his sides. When he finally opened one eye, Jake saw his favourite breakfast waiting on a plate for him. Right in front of his nose lay a stack of pancakes with maple syrup slowly dripping down the sides. Two strips of crispy bacon had been neatly tucked at their side, and a tall glass of ice-cold milk was just starting to bead with condensation.

"Breakfast is the most important meal of the day," his mom said, sitting down with her coffee. "And since this is an important day, you should eat up."

Jake thought about all the breakfasts his mom had made him, and how she knew exactly when he needed encouragement. Suddenly, he was hungry. He started in on the most important breakfast of his summer.

"Remember, just play the best you can," his mom said, watching Jake polish off his last bite. Jake knew that was all he could do. He just hoped his best would be good enough.

After putting his dishes in the sink, Jake got dressed, brushed his teeth, grabbed his golf bag, and went next door. Randy was already outside.

"I don't think I slept at all last night," he said, yawning.

"Me either." Jake's nightmares were still scary-real in his sleepy brain. "Maybe the walk to the clubhouse will wake us up." They set off down the street, trudging with their full golf bags slung over their shoulders.

Jake and Randy walked around the corner of the Royal Calgary clubhouse and stopped short at the mass of people. Jake had never seen so many junior golfers all in one place. He and Randy snaked their way through the crowd over to the Junior Club Championship scoreboard posted on a big wooden easel outside the Pro Shop. There were thirty-two names listed on the card, all written in big black letters. The names had been divided into eleven groups — ten threesomes and a single twosome listed by itself at the bottom.

Each group had a tee-off time marked beside it. The boys picked their way to the front of the pack to study the list more closely.

"I'm playing at nine-twelve with Brandon and Zach," Randy said. He ran his finger down the names until he found Jake's name — right at the bottom of the list. "And you're playing with … " Randy stopped as if to make sure his eyes were reading the name correctly. "You're playing in the very last group with TJ at nine-thirty-six. And it's only the two of you!"

It was true. Jake had been paired with TJ in the final group of the Championship. Everyone knew TJ was the best junior golfer at Royal Calgary. He had won the tournament the last two years in a row. How had Jake ended up matched against TJ? Jake wasn't sure, but he had a suspicion that Cliff might have had something to do with it.

"I bet this was Cliff's idea," Randy said, echoing Jake's thoughts. "Hey, at least it'll be easy for you to keep an eye on how your main competition is doing!"

Every player in the tournament had a chance of winning by shooting the lowest round on eighteen holes, but everyone knew TJ would have the score to beat.

All along, Jake had hardly admitted to himself that he wanted to do well in the Championship for one reason — to prove something to TJ. And now they were going up against each other. Jake was a bundle of nerves. He had never played all eighteen holes before. Now he was about to go head-to-head with TJ! Jake tried to relax by doing some stretching exercises to warm up, but his muscles felt stiff from all the tossing and turning in his bed the night before. *Maybe putting on the practice green will help me chill out*, he said to himself.

Jake carried his bag over to the green, then pulled out his putter and a couple of balls. But he was so tired and nervous, he forgot what Cliff had taught him. Instead of aiming at a tee, he started by putting right at the holes. The results were disastrous. Every hole looked as small as a dime. His putts were either too short or too long, too far to the left or too far to the right. Not a single one dropped into the cup. Jake shuffled away from the putting green, wondering what he was doing in the tournament at all.

He glanced over at the first hole and saw TJ swinging a club on the tee box to keep loose. TJ looked relaxed and confident. It was after nine-thirty, and all the other groups had teed off. Now it was just the two of them. The game was about to begin.

"Okay, boys, you can play away," Cliff announced, looking down the 375-yard fairway to make sure it was all clear. "Since TJ won the Championship last year, it's his honour — he gets to hit first."

TJ narrowed his eyes at Jake. "Good luck, Cooper. You're going to need it." He teed up his ball, took one last smooth practice swing with his driver, then hit it smack down the middle of the fairway. "You can expect to see plenty more of those," TJ boasted with a confident smile.

It was Jake's turn. He knew he should have warmed up more, especially since he was going to be hitting Cliff's driver for the first time. His palms were sweaty, his heart beat faster, he felt a little dizzy, and, when he bent over to push the tee into the grass, he just about fell over. Jake stood up, took a couple of shaky practice swings, then swung at the ball, hoping for the best.

But the best isn't what Jake saw. His ball did go straight down the fairway, but it hardly left the ground. It skidded about 50 yards through the thick grass. Jake hadn't teed the ball up high enough for the big driver, and had only hit the top part of it.

"Play fair and square, boys," Cliff warned, as Jake and TJ picked up their bags and started to walk down the fairway of the first hole. It was game on.

Jake didn't have to walk far to reach his lame first shot. The green was still more than 300 yards away, and he thought he could get back on track with a solid second shot. Jake pulled out his three-iron and took his stance in front of the ball. *Time to settle down,* he said to himself. He made a couple of practice swings, took a deep breath, then hit the ball. It flew straight for a second, then curved left toward the trees. A duckhook! This was worse than Jake's nightmare. This was for real.

Jake had taken two shots and he still hadn't reached TJ's first drive. Not only that, he was in the woods! Luckily, he found his ball and was able to chip back onto the fairway. Another three-iron shot, and his ball was sitting just in front of the green.

TJ was playing like a pro. His second shot had

sailed through the sky, landing 20 yards short of the green before rolling up onto the smooth putting surface. He had a chance for a one-under-par birdie.

On his fifth shot, Jake took dead aim at the flagstick and made a short chip shot. It headed straight for the flagstick, but Jake had hit it too hard. The ball rolled 10 feet past the hole.

Jake watched as TJ lined up his putt. It wasn't everyday a junior player had a chance for a birdie. TJ studied every break in the green from where his ball lay 30 feet from the hole. Finally, he was ready. His putt headed straight toward the middle of the cup, then broke to the right at the last second, coming to a stop just a foot away from the hole. He tapped the ball in for an impressive par four.

Jake still had a chance for a double-bogey six — two shots over par. He just had to make this putt. He stared at the hole, but it seemed to shrink by the second. If only he had practised putting at the tee. He made a smooth stroke, but his ball came up 6 inches short of the cup. He tapped it in. Jake and TJ walked off the first green together, but their scores were far apart.

"Don't worry, Junkyard Jake," TJ said snidely. "There are only seventeen holes to go."

Jake didn't say a word. What could he say? The scorecard said it all.

PLAYER	SCORE
TJ	4
JAKE	7

The rest of the front nine — the first nine holes, went pretty much the same for Jake. TJ kept calling him Junkyard, and Jake was zigzagging down every hole, chasing his ball from one side of the fairway to the other. He did manage to hit a few good shots, but not enough to keep pace with TJ.

And TJ was still playing like Tiger. The ball was going right down the centre of the fairway with every drive. His short iron shots were landing near the flagsticks. And his putting was bull's-eye accurate. Jake didn't think anyone could have played any better.

As the rivals walked off the ninth green, Jake saw his dream of winning the Championship start to fade away. He took out his pencil and scribbled down their scores for the front nine. TJ had fired a blazing 40, while Jake struggled to shoot 49. Jake was down by nine shots with only nine holes to play. For Jake to win, it was going to take more than just a few good shots. It was going to take a miracle.

17 Story Time

The competitors had a fifteen-minute break before they started the back nine — the last nine holes. That was just enough time for Jake to grab a sandwich and a drink. He trudged up to the snack bar at the clubhouse, where he found Cliff eating.

"How did you play?" Cliff asked, already knowing the answer by the look on Jake's face.

"Don't ask," Jake said. He looked down at his shoes.

"How many shots are you behind?"

"Too many." Jake wondered if he should even play the back nine.

"And how many is too many?"

"Nine," Jake sighed.

"Nine shots? That's nothing. In fact, it reminds me of a story that might make you feel a bit better." Jake was convinced that Cliff knew more about golf than anyone — even more than the magazines or the writers of *How to Play Like a Pro*. If he had a story about a golfer making a big comeback, Jake wanted to hear it. He listened closely.

"A few years back," began Cliff, "there was a young golfer who thought he was pretty good. Let's call him Cliff Spencer. He was so good he turned pro at an early age, thinking that he'd win every championship he entered. But it didn't happen. Not by a long shot. He travelled from tournament to tournament, all across the country. He played as hard as he could. But the harder he tried, the worse he got. After a while, his savings started to run out. He needed to win some prize money to keep playing on the tour. But when your name is at the bottom of the leaderboard, you're not winning very much money, certainly not enough to pay for expenses like meals and hotel rooms. After a while, Cliff felt like giving up. He thought that maybe golf just wasn't the game for him. So, he quit playing golf and got a job selling used cars."

Jake was amazed that Cliff would tell him such a personal story. How could he be so calm when he talked about giving up golf? Jake listened as though his life depended on it, and Cliff continued.

"Then one day, the guys from the car dealership where he worked decided to go golfing. They invited him along, not knowing he was an ex-professional. At first he didn't want to go, but they kept asking, so he agreed to play. And a funny thing happened when he did play. He had a great time. He joked with his friends. He was relaxed. He swung loose. And he played … like a pro. This made him realize what the problem was. He was putting too much pressure on himself.

"So, our boy Cliff stopped selling cars and started playing golf again. The first tournament he entered was thirty-six holes played over two days. He was rusty from his layoff and, after the first round, he found himself a whole lot of shots behind the leader. Nine shots to be exact. But you know what? It didn't bother him a bit. He went out the next day, calm as a summer breeze, and shot 63. It was the best round of his life. He finished first, but he didn't win any prize money."

"He didn't?" Jake was following Cliff's story as if he was in a trance.

"Nope. He won a new car."

"And I bet it was black," Jake laughed. Cliff had won the same car that "introduced" him to Jake, and he was still driving the prize.

Suddenly, Jake did feel a lot better. He realized he was still putting too much pressure on himself. No matter how many times Cliff told him to relax more, it wasn't easy to take it easy. But suddenly it was like a big weight had been lifted from Jake's shoulders. He sat up straighter at the counter, his eyes brightened, and his smile came back. He felt strong.

As Jake finished the last bite of his ham sandwich, Cliff offered one final piece of advice. "Remember, there's a reason why they don't award the trophy on the eighteenth fairway. You still have to putt on the eighteenth green."

Jake nodded and walked confidently out of the clubhouse. He picked up his bag and carried it over to the practice green. He still had a couple of minutes before teeing-off, and now he knew how to make the most of them. He pulled a white tee out of his pocket and stuck it in the green. Then he lined up three balls about 20 feet away and putted them with slow, smooth strokes, rolling each one toward the thin piece of wood. The last ball hit the tee dead on. Jake was ready.

18 Showdown

Jake walked briskly up to the tenth tee to find TJ lying on the bench. Instead of taking practice swings, TJ had decided to take a snooze.

"We've got some golf to play," Jake announced. The sight of TJ lying there fuelled his drive to outplay his opponent. "You won the last hole, so it's your honour."

"And I'm going to win the rest, too," TJ boasted, pretending to yawn while he stretched. "Yup, having my name engraved on that trophy for the third year in a row is going to be pretty sweet."

The tenth hole was a short but tricky par three. TJ and Jake stood on the elevated tee and looked down across a deep ravine to the green, 175 yards away. The fairway was lined with large poplar trees and the green was guarded by ball-swallowing sand traps on three sides. There was hardly a puff of wind as TJ stepped up to his ball. Jake watched him choose a four-iron from his bag and tee-off without even a practice swing. TJ made a smooth swing and froze at the top of his follow-through, like he was posing for the cover of *Golf Magazine*. He didn't even watch the ball, convinced he had hit a good shot. But Jake saw that he hadn't. The ball sliced like a big yellow banana and sailed into the beach-sized sand trap on the right side of the green.

Jake was up. He unfolded the small piece of rumpled paper he had brought on his practice rounds with Randy. He had scribbled down *175–3*. He decoded the numbers and pulled out a three-iron, knowing that if he hit it well, he could make the ball fly exactly 175 yards.

Jake took a few relaxed practice swings, then stepped up to his ball. *Thwack!* The ball took off from the hard steel face of his three-iron and soared through the cloud-dotted sky. The shot was headed straight at the flagstick, but Jake wondered if he had hit it far enough. Plummetting back to earth, Jake's ball landed just in front of the green and rolled up onto the putting surface, curling toward the flagstick. When it finally came to a stop, Jake's ball was just 10 feet from the hole. He pumped his fist in the air. This was how he knew he could play! If TJ was going to win the Championship, he was going to have to beat Jake to do it. And Jake wasn't going to make it easy.

TJ dug his spiked golf shoes into the loose sand and

looked up. He was standing deep in the trap, with the grassy lip of the bunker hanging straight above him. It was going to be a tough shot. TJ drew back his sand wedge and blasted. *Thud!* His ball sprayed out of the sand, but it hit the top edge of the trap and trickled back down to where he stood. TJ grimaced. "I can't believe it!" he shouted with frustration. TJ swung at his ball again. This time it launched out of the trap and onto the green, taking a large scoop of sand along with it.

TJ climbed out of the bunker, muttering under his breath. His ball was still about 20 feet from the flagstick. He was farther from the hole than Jake, and would play first. He lined up his downhill putt and stroked the ball. It headed toward the hole, gathering speed as it went. It rolled along, not slowing down, not stopping until it was 5 feet past the cup. TJ stomped over, almost pushing Jake out of the way. Even though it was Jake's turn to play, TJ couldn't wait to finish playing the hole.

"Okay if I putt out?" TJ asked, not waiting for a response.

"Take your time," Jake said, knowing TJ was so steamed that he would rush anyway.

TJ leaned over his ball and quickly putted. Instead of falling into the cup, the ball hit the edge of the hole and spun around the rim, ending up just outside the hole. TJ tapped his ball the remaining 6 inches, picked it up out of the hole, and stormed to the edge of the green to wait for Jake. Jake knew a triple-bogey six on a par three hole wouldn't make anybody happy — especially TJ.

Jake had 10 feet left for a birdie. He walked around his ball, studying all the angles. He took a couple of practice strokes, then putted. The ball rolled smoothly toward the cup, but curved left just before it reached the hole. Jake knocked his ball in the last foot. He shook his head, disappointed that he hadn't read the break properly, and had missed his chance for a birdie. But he had made a solid par. More importantly, with TJ shooting three over par, Jake had made up the three shots he lost on the very first hole of the tournament. He wrote down their scores and smiled. The tables were turned.

PLAYER	SCORE
TJ	6
JAKE	3

Now the two boys were on Jake's turf. TJ may have been a member of Royal Calgary, but no one knew the last nine holes better than Jake did. Jake and Randy had played every hole of the back nine almost a hundred times. And all those lessons from Cliff had been transmitted straight from Jake's memory to his swing.

Jake continued to chip away at TJ's lead. He picked up a stroke on hole number twelve, another on his favourite lucky thirteen, and one each on fourteen, fifteen, and sixteen. No matter what score TJ shot, Jake was one better. By the time the two competitors walked off the seventeenth green, Jake had caught TJ. There wasn't a stroke of difference between them. They were dead even.

It all came down to the eighteenth hole — one final challenge to determine who would be named the best junior golfer. Jake felt the pressure, and he knew TJ felt it too. They stood-side-by-side in silence on the last tee box. The only sound was the breeze rustling through the aspens. Both boys were too focused to speak.

The eighteenth hole stretched 400 yards ahead of them. It was the most challenging par four on the whole course. Jake and TJ had to drive over a creek, then hit up a steep hill to a green in front of the clubhouse. Even from where they stood, they could see a group of spectators already starting to ring the green in anticipation of their arrival.

The rivals stood staring down the fairway for a long time before TJ finally broke the silence. "Your honour, Cooper." Jake had won the honour on every one of the last eight holes, and had started to understand the full meaning of the word "honour": even if TJ didn't respect Jake as a person, he had to honour the fact that Jake was playing well. Hearing the words out of TJ's mouth made Jake feel strong. Was this confidence?

All Jake needed was one last good drive. He pulled out the big driver, its gold-coloured head gleaming in the sunlight. He reminded himself that this was the same driver Cliff had used to win his tournament when he returned to playing pro. Jake made sure he teed-up his ball high, and took a few steps back to survey the tree-lined fairway. It was long and narrow, with no room for error.

Jake took two sweeping practice swings and visualized the spot where he wanted his ball to land. He lined himself up, took a deep breath, then pulled back the head of his driver like an archer pulling back his bow. At the top of his backswing he paused for a split second, gathering all his strength before uncoiling a powerful downswing. *Thwack!* The driver crushed the ball right in the centre of the clubface. It soared straight as an arrow, splitting the fairway right down the middle. Jake could feel a surge of adrenaline. He must have crunched the drive more than 200 yards! He even heard TJ let out a gasp.

Jake knew he had left TJ an almost-impossible act to follow. But he also knew that TJ wasn't about to lie down and lose without a fight. Jake watched as his opponent punched his tee into the ground, then stood back and made two strong practice swings. TJ narrowed his eyes with steely determination and zeroed in on the ball. Then he let it rip. TJ's drive zoomed through the air before coming down on the left side of the fairway some 20 yards short of Jake's. It was a big-time drive, but it still left TJ with a long second shot to reach the green.

Studying the position of the balls, Jake didn't think TJ could make it to the green with just an iron. TJ must have been thinking the same thing. Jake looked over to see TJ pull a three-wood from his bag — a club that TJ hadn't used all day. *There's no way that will work,* Jake said to himself. But they both knew it was TJ's only chance to drive the ball far enough.

TJ settled himself over the shot and fired. His ball started out low but kept hurtling forward. It landed halfway up the hill, then bounded up the slope before trickling onto the putting surface. A big smile suddenly appeared on TJ's face, and he shot a glance at Jake as if to say, "*Take that!*"

Jake's ball sat nestled in the grass 175 yards from the green. *Time for a little more three-iron magic,* said Jake to himself. He pulled the trusted old club from his bag and took two practice swings. Then he took dead aim at the red flag and unleashed a relaxed yet powerful swing. His ball soared high over the hill to land softly on the fringe of the green, rolling gently onto the smooth surface.

The huge gallery of spectators whistled and applauded

wildly as Jake and TJ trudged up the steep slope to the eighteenth green. All the competitors except these final two had finished playing their rounds. Cliff had marked their scores on the Championship scoreboard and moved it to the side of the green. Everyone could see that it came down to just Jake and TJ. But there could be only one winner.

Randy stood in the crowd and cheered for his friend. "You can do it, Jake!"

A few steps away Brandon, Ryan, and Zach stood together rooting for the leader of the Fearsome Foursome. "You can take him, man!"

On the far side of the ring, two figures stood watching the final showdown of the tournament. One was a woman with short brown hair, her face tense with worry, her hands clasped hopefully against her chest. The other was a tall man, his skin tanned by hours of giving golf lessons under the hot sun. Jake's mom and Cliff looked on as the drama unfolded before them.

The crowd was buzzing as the two boys stalked around the green, sizing up their putts. TJ's ball was slightly farther from the flagstick, so he would play first. The putt was a 50-foot downhill monster that broke to the left. Jake figured TJ had about as much chance to sink his putt as Jake did to drop his own 40-foot twister. Just getting their balls close to the hole would be good efforts.

Jake waited his turn at the edge of the green as TJ bent over his ball to give it one last look. The crowd fell silent as TJ stroked his putt. The ball started out slowly, 6 feet to the right of the flagstick, then gained speed and spun down the hill, curving ever closer to the hole. The distance was almost perfect, and the ball came to a gentle stop less than a foot away from the cup. The gallery roared its approval. TJ smiled, soaking up the applause.

TJ's short tap-in for a par was probably good enough for at least a tie — Jake had almost no chance to sink his own impossible shot. Jake's putt had two big bends. The line to the cup looked like a long, twisting snake. Jake stood over the ball and took three slow practice strokes. Then he closed his eyes. He imagined that the huge crowd watching him didn't exist, that he was just on another morning mission with Randy, pretending to win the Masters Tournament. He remembered every one of Cliff's lessons, both on how to golf and how to be confident. He thought about how he had learned to trust friends like Randy and Cliff, and now to trust himself to make this long putt. One thing repeated in his head — *I can do this*.

The gallery held its breath as Jake pulled his flatstick back and stroked the ball. It rolled smoothly, first to the left, then to the right, before heading straight for the hole. With only a few feet to go, the ball started to lose steam and slow down. Jake could almost count each revolution of the ball as it inched its way to the cup. It wasn't going to make it! For a moment that seemed like an eternity, the ball hung on the lip of the hole, suspended in time and space. Then, it … dropped!

Jake punched the air with a huge uppercut as an even bigger smile flashed across his face. The crowd exploded with a thunderous cheer. Jake had done the undoable. He had birdied the final hole. He had beat TJ by a single stroke. Jake was the new Junior Club Champion at Royal Calgary! He stared at his scorecard, dreading that the numbers would change before his eyes. But there it was:

PLAYER	TOTAL
TJ	90
JAKE	89

Jake knew he would keep the scorecard forever.

When TJ saw Jake's ball fall into the cup, his first reaction was shock. But then he turned and rushed straight for his opponent. He carried a fierce look on his face and a putter in his fist. Jake looked up, alarmed. For a long moment, TJ loomed over Jake. Then he finally spoke.

"You got lucky, I guess," TJ said, grudgingly. As he turned away, he whispered to himself, "I should have won."

Jake's mom rushed up and gathered Jake in a big hug. Randy kept high-fiving the hand Jake had wormed out of his mom's arms, and Cliff just stood back and smiled. Jake watched as TJ stormed off the green and the rest of the Fearsome Foursome gathered around their one-time leader. There was anger in their accusing voices, and a hint of fear in TJ's eyes.

"I can't believe you choked!" Ryan shouted.

"Did you lose on purpose?" Brandon asked.

"You embarrassed all of us!" Zach shrieked.

As Jake stood in the middle of the green receiving the championship trophy from Cliff, he realized it had been a long time since he had envied TJ for anything — his money, his golf membership, his clothes, his friends who were now turning on him. Jake would take his family, his friends, and lessons from a real pro any day. As long as he had those things — and golf — how could he lose?

How to Play Like a Pro

Learn the lingo!

Just like other sports, golf has a lot of special words to describe the game. Here are some that will help you enjoy reading this book more.

Back nine: The last nine holes on a golf course

Birdie: A good score of one shot under the par for a hole

Bogey: A score of one over the par for a hole

Bunker: A large, deep hole filled with sand on the fairway or beside the green; see *Sand trap*

Chip: A short shot hit low to the ground that rolls onto the green

Clubface: The metal surface where the club strikes the ball

Clubhouse: The building at a golf club that holds the Pro Shop, locker rooms, and restaurant

Cup: The hole on the green

Dogleg: A hole with a corner bending to the left or right

Draw: A good shot that only has a small curve; the curve is to the left when hit by a right-handed player

Driver: The largest of the wood clubs, played off the tee and used to hit the ball farther

Driving range: A special fairway where players

practice drives and iron shots. Also called a "practice range"

Duckhook: An extreme hook that curves sharply like the flight of a duck; a duckhook veers left when hit by a right-handed player

Eagle: A great score of two under the par for a hole

Fairway: The short cut grass between the tee and green

Flag: The flag on top of the flagstick that marks the hole location

Flagstick: The slender pole with a flag on top that's placed inside the cup to mark the hole

Flatstick: Another name for a putter

Follow-through: The finishing position of a golf swing

Front nine: The first nine holes on a golf course

Gallery: Spectators

Green: The very short grass a player putts on to sink the ball in the hole

Hazard: A sand trap, lake, or stream that players try to avoid

Hook: A bad shot that has a big curve; the curve is to the left when hit by a right-handed player

Irons: Clubs made of steel, numbered two to nine, that hit the ball different distances

Leaderboard: The scoreboard that shows the list of leaders in a tournament

Line: The path the ball rolls on when hit at the cup

Par: A set number that shows how many strokes a good player would take to finish the hole

Power cart: A small, powered cart that carries two players and their bags while they play

Pro: The golf professional who manages the Pro Shop and gives lessons

Range cart: A small, powered cart that scoops up balls from the driving range

Rough: The long grass beside the fairway that players try to avoid

Sand trap: A large, deep hole filled with sand on the fairway or beside the green; see *Bunker*

Slice: A bad shot that has a big curve; it curves to the right when hit by a right-handed player

Tap-in: A short putt that is sure to put the ball in the hole

Tee: A piece of wood on which the ball is placed before teeing-off

Tee box: The area at the start of each hole where a player first hits

Top: To take a bad swing where the club only hits the top of the ball

Wood: A club with a large flat metal head used to hit the ball far